CROOKED TALES

Deception & Revenge in 15 Short Stories

Edited By

READERS CIRCLE OF AVENUE PARK

All the characters, companies, and organisations in this book are fictitious, and any resemblance to actual persons, living or dead, is purely coincidental.

The Authors have asserted their rights under the Copyright, Designs and Patents Act 1988 to be identified as the authors of this work.

All rights reserved. No part of this publication may be reproduced, stored in a retrieval system, or transmitted, in any form by any means, electronic, mechanical, photocopying, recording or otherwise, without the prior permission of the publishers.

This book is sold subject to the condition that it shall not, by way of trade or otherwise, be lent, re-sold, hired out or otherwise circulated without the publisher's prior consent in any form of binding or cover other than that in which it is published and without a similar condition including this condition being imposed on the subsequent purchaser.

Cover artwork by M.J. Fine
Picture Credits: Creative Commons/CCO StockSnap.io

First published by Copyright © 2017 Readers Circle of Avenue Park
All rights reserved.

ISBN-10: 1544057792
ISBN-13: 978-1544057798

ACKNOWLEDGMENTS

Our thanks to the editorial team, Geoff & Joseph—and the readers of READERS CIRCLE OF AVENUE PARK for their untiring efforts in curating this unique short story anthology. It was a global effort, literally, with authors contributing across several time zones that extended from Africa, Europe, Great Britain, and the United States.

To retain this distinctive international *flavor* (or 'flavour') each story is in the English style of its author, so some stories are in British English, some in American, and some reflect the jargon of a region.

The views and opinions expressed in this literary work are those of the author(s) and do not necessarily reflect the views or opinions of the READERS CIRCLE OF AVENUE PARK editorial team.

For more Short Story reading thrills, get the first edition of the 'Tales' series titled TWISTED TALES—direct from *Readers Circle of Avenue Park* or Amazon.com.

―――――

www.ReadersAvenuePark.weebly.com
Twitter: @ReadersAvePark   Hashtag #RCAP

CONTENTS

13	DEATH OF A SPARROWMAN	Eric J. Gates
28	A CROOKED MILE	Fiona Quinn
50	SQUATTER	Ulla Håkanson
58	NOTHING BUT THE TRUTH	Joseph Mark Brewer
65	ANGEL HEART	Michelle Medhat
100	THE SCREAM OF SILENCE	Pamela Crane
124	MARK OF THE HYENA	Mark Fine
143	BENEATH	Anita Kovacevic
160	UBIQUITOUS	Geoff Nelder
169	KEEPING IT IN THE FAMILY	Traci Sanders
179	SET FOR SATURDAY	Keith Dixon
186	COLD	Lubna Sengul
192	CONFESSIONS	Julie M. Brown
203	TERRESTRIAL TRAITOR	Jeremy Croston
223	RED QUEEN CHECK	Elizabeth Horton-Newton
238	*ABOUT THE AUTHORS*	

"Short stories consume you faster. They're connected to brevity. With the short story, you are up against mortality. I know how tough they are as a form, but they're also a total joy." - **Ali Smith**

"All Hail the Short Story"

The dreaded carpool lane at the local elementary school. Halftime during the Saturday-morning kids' soccer game. Waiting room anxiety at the doctor's office. Always waiting and often alone. You know these empty moments, well. These start-stop moments should be filled with life's rich stories...

Fill Life's Micro-Moments with Brief Tales

Life is now lived at breakneck speed. We need a breather. It's time to relax and indulge in a personal act of pure escapism—by enjoying a short story. Why not fill in life's micro-moments with brief tales of do-or-dare and make time's dull intervals even more enriched. For us, the twenty-first-century literati, the short story is the ideal narrative form. In fact, it is cool to be **#ShortStoryHip** in this hashtag world.

Satisfaction of a Full Story (but with fewer words)

Despite fewer words, the journey into the imagination is complete, as is the satisfying story arc and memorable characters. For the curiosity tempted, no longer the slow slog to reach a story's end—within a dozen pages or so the final twist in the tale awaits. Repeat. With a short story, no advance peeking at the "The End" page required as gratification is almost instantly satisfied.

Enrich Relatable Experiences with Short Stories

With a Smartphone, eBook, or paperback easily at hand, it is easy to read, anywhere. Let us count real reading moments that fill the void of time otherwise wasted:

- Waiting on your cappuccino's slow barista...
  Taste the rich, full-bodied flavour of fantasy.
- The number nine bus is late again...
  Time to travel swiftly across the written page.
- Work is a relentless, chaotic hassle...
  Escape into the tranquil realm of romance.
- The plane flight's delayed yet another hour...
  Far-off lands sit instantly in your opened hands.
- Terrified at the drill-clutching dentist...
  Use that screeching fear to taste tales of terror.
- Drudgery of the dreary daily commute...
  Be spirited away on distant, exotic adventures.
- Alone and abandoned at lunch break...
  Enjoy the company of quirky comfy characters.
- Dullness of the desolate bathroom...
  Well, it is now considerably more interesting.
- After your lover leaves, finally...
  Relish the literary companions of great affairs.

You have the itch to read, but have only a long moment to indulge, so 'hail a short story!" and immerse yourself in brief adventures of the imagination. In these and other life-moments, the short story is an entertaining and thoughtful companion—a bite-sized dose of thrills, chills, passion, or humor.

Consider this tempting proposition—countless *more* stories enjoyed in *less* time by you, the voracious reader. Vibrant stories. Scary stories. Dreamy stories. Sexy stories. Smart stories. Provocative stories. Personal stories. Funny stories. All these tales—a collective of the human experience—uniquely told in vignette literary packages.

Ultimate Sampler of Exciting, Talented Authors

Eager to meet great writers? Well, the short story is the ideal medium to discover new favorites. A single folio of short stories is the perfect platform to display the literary craft of intriguing authors—as displayed here, in this deceitfully delicious *Crooked Tales* collection—where the unexpected happens, the crooked are wronged, and wrongs are righted.

"You want to read? Don't have the time. No worries. Pick up a collection of short story favorites."
- Editors, Readers Circle of Avenue Park

"When you read a short story,
you come out a little more aware
and a little more in love
with the world around you."

*- **George Saunders***

*****

1

DEATH OF A SPARROWMAN

Eric J. Gates

A single figure, male, sitting on a park bench.

A few others braved the harsh northern wind to stroll among the leafy lanes and green islands that made up the Botanischer Gardens in Frankfurt's Grüneburgpark on this unseasonal end of Spring day. Only one was directly of concern to the seated figure bundled in the heavy overcoat. Others might be, should they show undue, and unwelcome, interest in what was about to happen.

The grays and browns were his domain. Inwardly he pined for the splashing colors of warmer climes. Yet the insipid tones filling his existence were an essential part of survival. Even his name, Don, spoken with an impossible soft "d," seemed to suggest it was over, nothing to worry about. Don, Dun, Done. The last time it had been used in

full had been on his Birth Certificate. His parents had always used the abbreviation. It was as though his conception had been a moment in an otherwise dull existence and now it was... done.

The object of his interest approached, hunched in a dirty, dark yellow worker's jacket and flat cap. Sly eyes scanned the surroundings for danger. This had to go smoothly for all. Anything else could, would, mean disaster and perhaps death. Not a quick, efficient demise either. An everlasting suffering for a captured agent under torture awaited those who took shortcuts in this game.

He had been, of course, an only child; he had been, of course, a lonely child. Incapable of surmounting the invisible barriers isolating him from his peers. Unaware of the meaning of friendship, and alien words like "share," "hug," and "love." It shaped him throughout youth into maturity. It became a trait, then an asset, one that curiously made him so good at his job. Proudly, some would call him "the man who wasn't there"; the most outstanding courier in the history of the Service. Not even a double-take would look at him twice. He **was** *smoke and shadows, skulking in a netherworld normal people ignored. Bland, he would say, happily. Blandly blending below anyone's radar. The spooks' spook. The consummate agent.*

The seated man, Don with a soft D, extracted a filled pipe from his overcoat. He never smoked, had not picked up the habit, perhaps from the lack of socializing and peer pressure in his youth. Now he found the disposable lighter

and, after a last, lingering look around, proceeded to puff the pipe into life. He fought the urge to cough, instead concentrating on making as much smoke as possible. This was the signal the strolling man awaited.

It was a complete mystery how a man like Don came to the attention of the Secret Intelligence Service, the Firm to its insiders, in the first place. The truth, as is often the case, was rather dull. He answered an advertisement for staff in a London newspaper. He passed all the aptitude tests and scored well on the IQ evaluation. Even his academic results were pleasing to the selectors. Yet where he failed, what eventually made him an ideal candidate for a covert courier, was simply the fact the selectors forgot about him as soon as he left their presence. He was such a gray individual; his very ordinariness was an asset. At least in the business of conveying confidential communications to agents in the field. He stood out... by not standing out.

He waited until the walker was some twenty strides away, then took the smoldering pipe from his mouth and tapped the bowl on the edge of the seat, as though settling the contents. The final gesture that all appeared safe to continue. The workman wandered past Don, showing no interest. As though subconsciously prompted by the fragrant fumes of the seated man's pipe, he removed a pack of cigarettes from an inside pocket.

He flicked out a white cylinder and a disposable lighter, then clicked the latter repeatedly, interspersing impatient shakes, as the object refused to collaborate. He halted his forward motion and looked around, a last-minute attempt

at spotting surveillance, then walked back toward Don.

When Don started that particular chapter of his life, traffic to and from MI6 operators was intense. It was the mid-eighties. The Berlin Wall had yet to be torn down. Spies plied their trade throughout Europe and North Africa, Don's stomping ground, with resolute determination, each trying to capture the coup that would give their masters "the edge," whatever that was. Those were days of subtle politics, of nuclear threats and counter threats, of Roger Moore camping it up as James Bond in the cinemas. It was an era without the Internet. Private Internet service suppliers were starting to scratch their collective heads wondering if Joe Public would be interested in what they could offer. The technological prehistory. Push-button telephones were slowly gaining momentum in users' homes. HumInt, Human Intelligence, was in its heyday. And when information had been stealthily gleaned, stolen, or fabricated in some point of the globe, it had to travel back to Century House, the MI6 Headquarters building on Westminster Bridge Road. And it had to do so as quietly and unobtrusively as possible. Even approaching the twenty-two floor, glass and steel monstrosity that was Six's HQ was fraught with peril. Soviet spies hunkered down in bedsits in Pearman Street alongside and happily documented all the comings and goings, safe in the naivety of the times.

The walking workman, holding the unlit cigarette and the useless lighter in one hand, approached.

"Guten Tag. Haben Sie Feuer?"

Don stood, fishing out his own lighter, an identical

match to the one the German-speaker held. He clicked the flame into existence and the man cupped Don's hand as he neared his cigarette. Concealed by gloved hands and a plume of grateful smoke, the man's lighter dropped into Don's waiting palm as Don's own was deftly clasped between two fingers and moved to the man's pocket.

"Danke, mein Herr." He raised two fingers to the peak of his flat cap in a salute and continued his stroll.

Don resumed his seat, showing more interest in the gathering of the little gray birds that squabbled for the bread he had thrown at his feet than the receding form. The microSD cards hidden in the opaque bodies of both lighters were the prize that had been safely exchanged today. He would feed the birds for another few minutes before glancing at his wristwatch, then walking briskly away in the opposite direction in search of a taxi to the airport and the delivery of his prize to his masters in the UK. Job done.

Don, and the rest of the elite band of surreptitious shippers the Firm employed, were forever banned from approaching the building. After a recent security audit it had been declared "irredeemably insecure" and requests had been submitted for the construction of a new home for Britain's foreign intelligence service. Even when the Iron Lady approved the funding, the new monstrosity, nicknamed "Legoland" by its early inhabitants, was also off-limits. Someone had deemed a radius of a mile and a half was tainted territory. Thus Don was condemned to meeting his handlers in pubs, restaurants, shopping centers, railway stations, public lavatories and other odd places where the same 'someone' had decided safety existed. Don often

wondered if the sister agency, the Security Service, MI5 as it was popularly known, imposed similar restrictions on its own couriers. In their case it would probably result in a nightmare of no-go areas as the agency operated out of several buildings spread through the nation's capital. Or at least they did until "practical considerations," and not a little petty jealousy as "Six" was granted a brand spanking new building at Vauxhall Cross, triumphed. Then the unification of all in Thames House in Millbank, central London, the abandoned offices of Imperial Chemical Industries as it sold everything it could as part of survivalist reorganization, in the mid-nineties. That would make courier exclusion zones much easier to manage, thought Don.

Six days, three trips abroad. Don was tired. He knew his job was not physical; no leaping from moving cars or hand-to-hand fighting with enemy agents for him. The mental strain was what wore at him. The ever-present pressure of the exchanges being traps; of police or "the opposition" waiting to snag him and his contact. His initial training at the SIS's Fort Monkton conclave on Britain's south coast did not prepare him for that. Yes, they had given him basic skills with weapons, guns and knives, though had hastily added they never expected him to have to use them. Of late a hidden heaviness had formed within Don's psyche, perhaps an awareness so many years of trouble-free travel would be tempting the odds. He had taken precautions. Just in case. Simple precautions, yet they provided an anchor for his freewheeling, doom-laden thoughts. He caught himself fingering the thin hilt of the

long ceramic blade held against the underside of his left forearm by a single adhesive bandage, a talisman warding off ill-fortune, a good-luck charm out of place in the harsh reality of modern espionage. Then there was his own agenda, the preparations started years ago to provide for a future he hoped to enjoy.

Don loved his job; excelled at it. To maintain his cover, to hide the trips to collect or deliver "packages" throughout his assigned territory, Don had to travel constantly. Officially, openly, he was a freelance commercial representative. The bombastic title meant he was a wandering salesman of sorts, ever seeking the latest product to present to potential professional purchasers in Blighty. This meant almost every day he was hopping on trains and planes, occasionally driving, too, with the odd boat trip thrown it for variety, to conferences, fairs and exhibitions throughout the UK, Europe and Africa. Often these trips were merely cover to allow him to ply his trade as a glorified messenger. Other times they were simply sojourns whose number allowed the creation of the haystack wherein the needles would be lost to any casual observers, or not so indifferent scrutiny from rival agencies. He saw his role as one of a facilitator and puzzle-master. Working to help the flow of carefully gathered intelligence to and from his home country, and above all, never getting caught or compromising the agents he encountered. Those were his defining roles. Those were the pepper in his vodka. The sneaky snatch of a document left in a Dead Drop, the furtive fling of a package at a Car Toss, the fleeting physical conveyance of a Brush Pass. All these and more fed his

personal pride, yet none contributed to his future plans. They were a means to an end, just as they were for his employers.

The *end*, his *end*, came sooner than expected.

The twenty-first century had brought changes to the covert carriers. The Internet above all provided routes considered fairly secure for low-grade intelligence to be delivered through hidden host servers dotted around the globe. That left the really critical stuff; the most valuable product that had to be hand-delivered by Don and his sort. Fewer trips, but of greater worth.

Another journey. Another delivery. Yet another small electronic prize to convey, molded into the straps of a plastic carrier bag. This time in sunny Spain. He preferred the parks. They provided an opportunity to rest from the endless travel, to commune with nature and his particular following of feathered friends. The darting motions of the small birds always filled him with joy. He saw in them an analogy to his own function. Quick, decisive, fearless actions that, for the sparrows, gained the prize of the bread bits he pitched, and in his case, ensured his survival from foreign predators. This time the meet would be in the Retiro Park, the ebullient expanse sited in the heart of the capital city. It was now late May. A quick check of the Internet showed him the "Feria del Libro," the annual book fair, would be in full swing, filling a section of the park with almost four hundred stalls and millions of visitors during its two-and-a-half-week run. Plenty of cover for a covert conveyance.

Opportunity for escape too, should matters not go as expected. And for "the opposition," the prospect of using the agglomeration as cover for a sting. Perhaps agents from the Civil Guard, or the National Police; maybe operatives from the CNI, Spain's spy service. None would be good news, particularly this late in the game.

Now the only issue was the weather. May in Madrid meant anything goes. In theory, Spring should have been dictating the sun's presence in the sky. The comfortably warm days before the stifling heat of the Summer. But, that was the *theory*. Reality was cleverly encompassed by a rhyming Spanish saying: *"Hasta el cuarenta de Mayo no te quitas el sayo."* Until May fortieth, don't take off your smock. It lost a lot in the translation, but its truth was felt by the *madrileños* every year. The book fair had a reputation for being *"pasada por agua,"* waterlogged. As he strolled along the long row of bookstalls, his eyes ever vigilant, the sky above darkened. It was just a couple of tones; a downpour did not seem to be on the agenda just yet, but perhaps it presaged the later events.

It was still early for the crowds that would descend on the bookstalls seeking a bargain purchase or a dedication from their favorite scribe, but this still meant several hundred slow-moving individuals pressed against the facing rows of booths. Don kept to the center of the passage between the back of the masses huddled around each stall. This gave him decent cover while providing plenty of opportunity to look around. No suspicious people showed on his personal radar. No watchers waiting to snap him up. Don was aware the deliveries he was trusted to carry these days were always high-value intelligence. He knew this, so

did the opposition. A big trophy should they fall into the wrong hands. The element of danger implicit in his task was therefore acute too.

He glanced at his wristwatch. Not at the time, no; he was early for his meet. The date told him he had a little more than two years before his 'retirement plan' would run its course and he would undertake a final journey, a one-way trip, to a new future. It could not come soon enough as far as he was concerned.

Between the stalls, Don spied the bench he was supposed to use.

Someone was already occupying one extreme.

Could it be his contact had decided to turn up early too?

He did not like this.

No, this was not good.

He paused, analyzing his feelings. He felt he lost some degree of control by not being the first to his meetings.

He shook his head. He was letting apprehension get the better of him. His doctor had warned him about this. The last time, over two years ago now, he had even experienced a panic attack. It had been this that gave him the final push to develop his 'retirement plan', so some good had come out of the few minutes of hell he had suffered.

Two figures, male, sitting on a park bench.

As soon as Don sat, the sparrows started to land nearby, anticipating by some sixth sense perhaps he was here for them. Don smiled; a rare gesture. He avoided eye contact

with the other occupant of the bench as he extracted the used, yellow plastic bag from his coat pocket. The birds approached in expectant hops. Certainty was now theirs. The same could not be said for Don. As he extracted the bread roll purloined from the hotel's breakfast counter and started to tear it into sparrow-sized chunks, he used his peripheral vision to scope out the other man.

Young, maybe early-thirties. Hatless, hair longer than acceptable to Don. Eyes hiding behind dark glasses, unnecessary today under the gathering clouds. A beak-like nose, more at home on his feathered followers. He smiled to himself again. Yes, the man was a larger version of the gray and brown creatures squabbling at his feet. Hands, dangling in the air as elbows rested on the back of the bench. Long, weak fingers. A clunky steel watch half-hanging from a bony wrist. Clothes, unremarkable, nothing outstanding except for ... shoes, sneakers, bright blue with a lurid yellow stripe. They looked comfortable, thought Don. He didn't own anything like them. Sturdy, thick-soled brogues made up his own footwear, useful for someone who walked a lot at product fairs, and who, at a pinch, might have to kick someone hard if push came to shove.

The minutes passed. Don immersed in his feeding of the flock. Visitor glancing surreptitiously at his wristwatch.

Finally, the bench neighbor spoke.

It was not what Don had hoped to hear, the short, odd, out of context phrase identifying him as *the contact*. Don had already, with the display of the yellow plastic bag, shown it was okay to proceed.

"Good morning, Don. Nice to finally meet you." The phrase punctuated by a studious glimpse of the watch face.

Don was stupefied. He fought to maintain his attention on the birds as he digested the transgressions in his mind. He was not traveling under his real name. He never did. He had over forty fake identities backed up by Her Majesty's finest real passports, plus a few from other nations. It was bad tradecraft to refer to another agent by their real name in the field, even if you knew it, and in this case, today was the first time Don had seen the man seated at the other end of the bench.

"Oh, I'm sorry. Broke the rules there. No matter, though. In the context of today, it makes little difference."

Should he reply? Should he stand up and leave, with a final scattering of the bread to his flock, of course?

"I see you like feeding the birds. Not my thing, birds. Flying rats, most of them." The accent was Oxbridge. "Now, frogs, that's another matter."

His mind screamed 'run', yet the surreal nature of the situation cemented Don's rear to the bench.

"Frogs. Know anything about them?"

Don recognized the gambit for what it was. A way to force him to interrelate with the stranger. He chose silence. His eyes however betrayed his interest, fixing on the sharp nose and dark glasses of the man alongside.

"Four thousand, seven hundred and forty. Imagine that!" Another glance at the watch hanging loose from a thin wrist.

Don guessed what the figure meant.

"That's how many different species there are, and more being discovered. Not like your bloody sparrows, is it? How many species are they? Two, three?"

"Twenty-six." Don felt impelled to defend his avian fondness.

"Ah, he speaks! So, twenty-six it is. Still nowhere near my frogs though." A pause. A peep at the timepiece. "Not interested in all the species though. No. The run-of-the-mill croakers have no fascination for me. The ones I like are a subset, if you will. You see, I'm a biochemist."

Don couldn't help himself. He was now staring openly at the man. Was he going to hold out his hand in a gesture of greeting? Tradecraft had long abandoned the scene here.

"Yes. Biochemist. The ones I search out have a common characteristic. They can kill you." He chuckled; a dry cackle, a nasal honk.

"It took us a while to figure it out, you know." It was a statement, Don assumed. No reply necessary. The non sequitur bothered him.

"I work for the same Firm as you, Don. Odd that, I suppose. Here's me, a scientist, and you, a ... exactly what are you? A messenger of sorts, I suppose. A paltry postman for Her Majesty's secret agents. Doesn't sound a very interesting line of work to me." Another gander at the time. "Better get a move on. Ah, where was I? Oh, yes. It took us more than a year to work out it was you. Secrets being sold on the black market. What have you been doing? Copying your packages before delivery? Naughty, naughty. That's why we've been sending certain content through you of late. Made it easy to confirm our suspicions. Use you for disinformation. Until your effectiveness came to an end, that is. That's where I come in. Frogs."

This time the pause was much longer. Don could not see the man's eyes but he had the feeling they were turned inward. Something about time. Calculations. Don cast his gaze around the park seeking approaching individuals bent

on arresting him.

"Do you know there are some really intriguing frogs out there? There're a couple I came across in the Brazilian savannahs that can give you a nasty surprise. One of my colleagues touched one by accident and ended up in intense pain for almost six hours. He was lucky though. Had it have been the other one, he would be dead. A single gram of the skin excretion of *Aparasphenodon brunoi* can kill eighty adult men. Imagine that! Riveting, but bloody useless. No, what I was asked to do was alter the venom. Change its genetic markers so it could be administered safely to release its deadly potential at a precise time, after a certain number of hours have passed. Now *that* was a challenge."

This man is here to kill me, thought Don.

"Yes, difficult, but not impossible." Now he stared at the wristwatch. "It's been twenty hours since you took receipt of the latest package, hasn't it? Now, supposing you wanted to make your illicit copy as quick as you could, that means the poison has been working on you for, say, nineteen hours? Give or take. This isn't rocket science. In fact, you are the first field trial. I got tired of killing of mice and pigs. That's why I'm here personally. Had to be in at the finish, you see."

Don felt suddenly warm.

His face flushed with intense heat.

His temples throbbed as blood rushed through his arteries.

He felt a tightness across his chest.

A shortness of breath.

He gulped air into his lungs.

"If my math is spot on, the first symptoms should be

kicking in soon. Oh, you're probably wondering how I did it? Easy, really. I coated the small USB pendrive hidden in that plastic bag you picked up yesterday morning in London with my creation. Once it gets on your skin, that's it. Job done. Nano-tech. Brilliant, even if I say so myself. You killed yourself, really, when you took the pendrive out to copy it. So efficient!"

Don stood shakily, then stumbled toward the man.

In the blink of an eye, he thrust the thin ceramic blade into the soft skin under the jaw and up into the brain. A quick, unnecessary, twist. He stood.

The panic attack forced him to breathe hard, though he knew he would be okay. No frog venom for him. Something, his own sixth sense perhaps honed through years of covert work, had told him not to open this package, not to copy it. Trusting your own instincts, rule number one for a good spy. He glanced about, ensuring his actions had not attracted attention.

Don shrugged as he strolled unhurriedly away. Time to put his retirement plan into action.

He looked back over his shoulder.

A single figure, male, sitting on a park bench.

Slumped.

A cheeky sparrow perched on the seat alongside, pecking at the spilled breadcrumbs.

+++

2

A CROOKED MILE

Fiona Quinn

Gator looked at home with a flowered dishtowel tucked into the waistband of his tactical fatigues, doing KP at my sink. I sat at the table making up a grocery list, humming. All day long a nursery rhyme had been cycling through my brain. *There was a crooked man, who walked a crooked mile.* Often times, when I thought a rhyme or sang a refrain from a song, it was my subconscious chewing on something. Sometimes that something was out of my day-to-day life and sometimes it was something I was picking up on my psychic bandwidth, something out of the ether. It was impossible for me to tell which was which until a connection was made and the lights switched on with an "ah ha!"

I glanced down when Beetle and Bella, my Dobermans, jangled their tags as they lifted their heads on alert. Bella cracked the air with her sharp bark followed immediately by

a ring at the door. My gaze snagged on the clock; Missy showed up right on time.

Missy was thirty, but she looked like a teenager. She shrugged out of her over-sized coat and folded it neatly over the arm of my sofa. Her mousy brown hair was pulled back in a ponytail, making her hazel eyes look very large in her pale face. Her expression always had the pinch of worry with a little bit of sad mixed in. Her mouth was slow to smile, but when she did, it was a pretty smile.

"Can I get you a cup of coffee? Some tea?" I asked as I wandered back to the dining room, where I had a fire crackling. Today was one of the coldest I could remember. Moist and miserable, the temperature from the coming storm had followed Missy into my living room and trailed along with us as we moved farther back in my shotgun-styled house with its rooms lined up in a straight row: living room, dining room, kitchen.

"No thanks, Lexi, I'm good." She hustled over to the fire and reached her stiffened pink fingers toward the warmth.

My house was part of a duplex. My neighbor on the other side, Mrs. Nelson, had recently had a stroke and moved to an assisted living facility. I bought her house from her and now owned the whole building, though some updates and repairs would need to be made before I could rent out that space.

Mrs. Nelson could only take so much with her to the new and much more confined space, so she offered everything else to Missy to either use or sell, as she saw fit. Missy, the mom of three young kids, had run out of her house barefooted and pajamaed, saving herself and her

children from a brutal husband, now imprisoned. She moved here to my DC neighborhood where she was doing her best to make a new life for her family. Most everything Missy owned was from a church donation box or found on the side of the street with the trash, brought home, and renovated to make it serviceable if not exactly pretty.

Mrs. Nelson, gosh, I just thought so much of her for finding a way to help Missy out in such an amazing way and make it seem like it was Missy who was doing Mrs. Nelson the favor. Missy often had her back up. She didn't take charity, and she didn't abide pity. She was resilient. She wanted her children to see how to stand strong in the face of adversity. I loved that about Missy. She was a role model for me. But I was still glad things were going to be a little easier for her now. Neighbors helping neighbors, that phrase described my childhood. "We are our brothers' keeper," and "It takes a village," were the philosophies not only embraced by my parents but the whole small apartment complex I grew up in. Values I tried to embody every day as an adult.

Missy turned toward me. "I have a ton of boxes I've been saving from work in the trunk of the car. I thought maybe I could pack things up as I went through Mrs. Nelson's stuff. Make it easier in the long run."

"Sounds like a plan." I angled my chin toward the kitchen where I could hear Gator finishing up. That was our deal – I'd cook for him and his grizzly bear appetite, but he'd do the cleanup. "Gator, are you hanging out here? Or are you coming next door with us?"

"Gator?" Missy raised a questioning brow.

Gator sauntered out of the kitchen drying his hands on the dish towel. He looked like apple pie and Saturday

night football all rolled into one. He definitely made Missy perk up and take notice. I didn't blame her. Gator would stir any warm-blooded woman's interest, especially when he was dressed like he was, in his Iniquus uniform of camouflage BDUs and a gunmetal-grey compression shirt that showed off his washboard abs. Iniquus was a for-hire security group who contracted the best of the best as they left the military and entered the civilian world. Gator was a trained Marine Ranger. He was definitely best of the best. I worked on Gator's team, Strike Force, doing intelligence for Iniquus.

"He has a girlfriend," I whispered into Missy's ear, when I caught her speculative gaze focused on my teammate. "Gator, I'd like you to meet my next door neighbor, Missy. Gator's going to be living here while I get Mrs. Nelson's house fixed up; then, he's going to be living on the other side of my duplex." I laughed inwardly as Missy tried to untangle her tongue. Gator often had that effect on women. Finally, she nodded and shot her arm out to shake hands.

"Nice to meet you, ma'am. I'd be glad to help out," Gator spoke with a gumbo-rich accent warmed with the spices of the Louisiana bayou. As he moved to the closet to grab his jacket, I pushed Missy out ahead of me, to keep her from drooling on my rug.

Missy and I sat on the worn linoleum floor in Mrs. Nelson's kitchen, filling up boxes as fast as we could. Gator hefted them up on his massive shoulders and carried them up the street, stacking them in Missy's dining room to be sorted and put away later. We had the radio cranked up to boost our energy.

"What's that?" Missy asked.

I glanced over to see what she was referring to. She had her hands on her hips; her head canted to the side.

"What's this?" I held up a sixpence that I had found in a sugar bowl shaped like Big Ben.

"No. You keep mumbling. 'There was a crooked man, who walked a crooked mile.'"

I smiled at her, not sure what to say.

"You've been mumbling it under your breath since you started to wrap up those dishes."

"Yeah, do you remember how the rhyme goes?"

"Uh, let's see. . . There was a crooked man, who walked a crooked mile, he found a crooked sixpence upon a crooked style," she sing-songed.

"That's ironic. I got those words stuck in my head, and then I find this sixpence." I gave a half-hearted smile, putting the coin back in place and wrapping Big Ben in newspaper. To be honest, that coincidence had my psychic antenna on a swivel.

"There's more to the poem, isn't there?" I pulled my phone from my pocket and did a Google search. "Yup, it finishes: He bought a crooked cat, which caught a crooked mouse, and they all lived together in a very crooked house."

"And why are you thinking about that?"

Before I could answer, Gator sauntered in from moving the coffee table up the street. He rubbed his hands over his ears. "Whoo, that cold's got a mean streak. I think probably one more load, then I should take your pups on a quick jog, Lexi. It'll be a while before they can get out and get exercise again. What time are they saying Armageddon starts?"

"Around twenty-three hundred hours should be the height, but—"

I stopped when the radio sounded an alert signal. The alerts had been broadcasting all afternoon. There was one heck of a big storm moving into the DC area. Ice and treacherous winds would sweep down from the north. The temperatures would fall life-threateningly low. They expected the whole region to lose electricity for long periods and the roads to be impassable. The news reported runs on the stores; there was no more milk, bread, or toilet paper to be had in our area. If you were looking for a chain saw or a generator, you'd need to drive down to southern Virginia to find one still on the shelves. And if you headed down there, you might as well stay until DC thawed itself out.

Emergency shelters were opening so our homeless population and those who depended on electricity for warmth wouldn't freeze to death in the streets or in their unheated houses. I had a generator full of gas and plenty of wood stacked on my back porch. I was ready. But now they were announcing gridlock on the highways as much of Washington, DC, scrambled to get home and burrow in.

To my surprise, this announcement wasn't about the weather. "We are asking citizens in the Mont Blanc area to be on the lookout for an elderly man with Alzheimer's who wandered away from his caregiver earlier today. The two had walked up to Barnaby Market at Palmetto and Norton to pick up supplies for the storm when he disappeared. If you are in that area, please check to see if he entered your building, especially before locking up and heading home in advance of the storm. Contact local police if you should spot him."

The radio announcer went on to describe a tall thin man with black wool trousers, a black overcoat, a grey scarf and hat. He concluded by again counseling everyone to go home and stay home. "No one can drive on ice."

I checked my phone for missed messages. Normally, my search and rescue team would get a call out for such an event. I dialed over to Sid, my task force leader, to see what the status was and if they needed another pair of eyes. It was getting dark, and the temperatures were below freezing already. I was scared for this guy. Time was short for keeping him alive.

"We weren't called in, Lexi," Sid said.

"What? Why?" I paced anxiously across Mrs. Nelson's living room.

"They decided to use a FEMA urban search and rescue crew. With this storm moving in, they're worried about putting civilian volunteers in harm's way. They want everyone home and off the streets. The hazard level was red. We can't allow anyone out in the field."

I rubbed my palm across my forehead. "For this guy too. I'd say his hazard level is off the charts. Do you have any details?"

There was a long pause. "Lexi, I know you live near that area, but we don't deploy without being asked."

I pulled the drapes away from the window and stared up at the grey sky with its ominous clouds. "I hear you. But I'm about to take my dogs for a last run before the storm turns full force. Wouldn't hurt if I had a few more particulars."

Sid sighed. "I don't have anything else other than that his name is Bruce Walker."

"Huh," I said to no one in particular as I hung up. *There was a crooked man.*

"They aren't sending out rescue?" Missy asked.

"They, um. . ." *Who walked a crooked mile.* The rhyme was getting louder in my head. "Uh, they called in a FEMA team. They've got the search covered."

Gator tilted his head. "I thought USAR did structural collapse."

"It's the storm. They want people who work hazard for a paycheck instead of us volunteers."

Gator grinned. "So you're taking the dogs on a walk to Barnaby Market?"

"Yup. The girls and I might just need to bundle up and go on an adventure."

Gator's phone was out and pressed to his ear. "Hey Blaze, you and Deep wanna go on an adventure?"

As two more guys from our Iniquus team, Strike Force, headed over. I called my neighbor, Dave Murphy, to see if the Bruce Walker case happened to have landed anywhere near his detective's desk. I didn't think it would. This wasn't a crime. But, it would be nice to have a little information. And I knew that if I walked into the precinct and asked questions, they'd escort me right on back out the front door. Dave had nothing to add but he made a phone call to smooth the path for me when I showed up at the precinct. It was a good thing too because I was absolutely convinced that Bruce Walker's disappearance was the reason I had this darned nursery rhyme looping through my consciousness. It was my duty. I needed to get out there and find this guy.

Gator, my dogs, and I piled into the Humvee that Blaze and Deep had driven over. They were turned out in storm gear, and had brought Gator and me sub-zero clothing, as well. I dressed Beetle and Bella in thick, fleece-lined coats with Search and Rescue insignia and ID in case they ran after a scent; I wanted everyone to know they were at work. I had put their radio collars on and tested out the system. I handed one radio receiver to Gator; he'd monitor Beetle. I kept the other for myself to monitor Bella. I was holding off until the last minute to put on their doggy socks and booties – they *hated* them.

We tried to stop for fast food on the way to the police station but most everything was already closed. When we pulled up between two police cruisers, I left my teammates in the Hummer, and ran in to talk to Sergeant Schwarz.

"Hey Stan!" I gave him a big hug. Stan Schwarz was a lifelong family friend. "Long time no see."

"Good that you're getting involved here, Lexi. I'm real worried about this guy. We just got the newest weather report. I doubt he could make it 'til midnight, and from what I can see the urban search team is focusing one hundred percent on searching buildings." He stopped and pointed a finger. "But the second and I mean the *very* second even the teeniest tiniest particle of ice hits the ground, you go home. Got me?"

"I've got you." Midnight. My adrenaline spiked. I couldn't imagine how horrible it would feel to freeze to death. "You want to show me where Mr. Walker was last seen?" I walked over to the wall-sized map hanging in the briefing room.

Stan put his finger on the place where Walker had been with his caregiver. "They were leaving the store with their groceries. The caregiver sat Mr. Walker down on a bench then ran back into the store to let the manager know that there was broken glass on the sidewalk. When she came back out, he was gone. Geez she was a mess. I thought we were gonna have to sedate her," he said, reaching behind the podium. "Here's his pillow case." He handed me a plastic Ziploc with a folded, blue pillowcase nestled inside. "The USAR isn't using K9s so I can give you this sample. Mr. Walker last had his bed changed a week ago, so it should be a good scent source. Only Walker and the caregiver have touched the pillow case." He reached into the file he had dangled from his other hand. "And here are a couple of photos and the list of places Dave asked for. It's all I got."

I took the things in my hand and looked them over. "We'll do our best. Was that the caregiver outside in the hall crying?"

"That's the granddaughter. She brought the photos over for her mom. The family's all out driving around looking for Walker, and the granddaughter's waiting for her boyfriend to show up in his four-wheeler, so they can go in a different direction. But we told them to get off the streets before the ice starts." He ducked his head and raised his eyebrows to make the point again that as soon as the danger began in earnest I'd need to give up the hunt.

"Okay. I'm just going to stand here and look at the map for a minute, get my thoughts together."

"You're fine. Take your time. Let me know if I can be any help — but anything I do's going to have to be unofficial. I'm not stepping on any toes over at FEMA and

Homeland Security. Now I've got to get back to my desk. You make sure to give me a call when you get home so I can stop worrying about you."

"You got it. Thanks, Stan."

As Stan walked out of the meeting room, I walked over to the map with a pencil in my hand. I put the point on the spot where Mr. Walker had been last seen.

I imagined being outside – the bitter cold, confusion, darkness. I could picture him panicking. I wondered if he thought that that night he was going to die, if he knew that he should be doing something to help himself, but he couldn't remember what it was that he should be doing, where it was he should be going.

I tried to hone in on him using my sixth sense. I waited for a direction and nothing came to me. What I did sense was that Mr. Walker didn't know how he had gotten to where he was. Things seemed to be in the wrong place and this confused him. He wasn't going to be much help to my search so I waited for his perceptual clues to come into focus. The first thing I became aware of was that there were no lights. At this time of day that meant no buildings, no street lights; he wasn't on a road. There were trees. There were dogs barking ... there was a woman talking. She was talking gibberish. The noise made Mr. Walker feel afraid. I listened to the gibberish, it sounded like the mutterings of a person with mental health issues, perhaps a homeless person who had been left in the park after rescue teams had done their transport to the shelters? I made a mental note to keep my eye out for her. She would need saving from the storm every bit as much as Mr. Walker. I sensed that Mr. Walker was trying to evade whomever it was that was chattering.

This was bad news. It was hard enough to find someone out in the open, but now Mr. Walker was escaping from someone. Escaping? Yes, that word felt right. There had been a physical struggle of some kind and now he was escaping.

I mentally pulled myself away from Mr. Walker. Since I wasn't going to be able to trace his path on the map, I looked to see if there were any green spaces around, where he could have wandered. Blaze walked through the door and sidled up beside me.

"Hey, things are starting to pick up out there. The temps are dropping like crazy. I came in to see if I could be any help. We need to get moving."

"Look at this Blaze, Stan was right. Mr. Walker went missing in a very urban area. There are lots of places for him to go in and get warm. Lots of people to see him, realize he's in trouble, and give the police a call. But with the storm, everything's closed. If he was inside somewhere, they'd have kicked him out. If he were going to be seen, he would have been seen by now. The family is driving around in separate cars hoping to catch a glimpse of him. I don't think he's in this area." I drew my finger in a circle around the last known location. "I think he's here." I pointed at a public garden; the only green space anywhere remotely nearby.

Blaze measured against the key at the bottom of the map. "Lexi, that's seven miles."

"I know. Most times people stay within a mile or two of where they were lost. There are a few things different here. Firstly, Mr. Walker is in the later stages of Alzheimer's. He's not thinking like you or I would think."

"Seven miles?" Blaze scratched his fingers through his copper-colored hair that tried desperately to curl, even though it was cut in a tight military buzz.

"He could easily have wandered seven miles since his disappearance. At any rate, look, this is his last known location. See? He'd have to have gone north or south on that road. Just to the north is the huge intersection. Noisy, confusing. I think he went south. If you follow the roads, you see how they'd make him flow in the direction of the park. People with Alzheimer's tend to walk in a straight line."

Blaze stood with his hands on his hips, looking at the map. He took his index finger and tried to trace out different routes. "That makes sense to me. I'll bet that's where he headed. This is gonna be like looking for a needle in a haystack. He could be anywhere, including locked up in some building somewhere. So, what's the plan?"

"I'm going to let Beetle and Bella try to pick up a trail. It's cold; that will keep the scent close to the ground, and the wind has been low so far today. They might be able to get something. It's been hours, and there's probably been a lot of foot traffic. Reality is it's a long shot. Maybe if they can even verify my idea about direction, it would be a help."

Beetle and Bella were thrilled to be off lead and on a scent. They almost never trained in an urban setting. I was going to have to pay close attention that they didn't pick up on something and run after it out into traffic. Though, thankfully, almost everyone had already headed home and the streets were all but empty. The Humvee let me off in

front of the market; Deep was driving. Blaze and Gator were with me on foot.

Sure enough, when I held the scent under their noses, the dogs went right to the bench where Mr. Walker had been sitting, and then took off to the south. Within the block, though, the scent trail went cold. I kept walking towards the park. Every once in a while, one of the dogs would pick up something, and signal a hit. We'd follow it along until the scent trail went cold again. Seven miles.

Seven miles when the temperatures were heading toward the single digits, with a wind that had been steadily picking up, and was now bending the trees, was hard core. Even dressed as we were, in ski pants and parkas, we all felt the pinch of cold as our noses ran and froze, and our fingers tingled and burned. I reached into my pack that Blaze had slung on his back, and got out hand and foot warmers to distribute. I slipped them under the dogs' work vests as well. The chemical heat took the edge off.

We slogged on. Knowing how painful it was to be out in this, and that Mr. Walker didn't have nearly the same amount of storm gear as we did, pushed me to fight harder to get to him. The gusting wind made us turn our backs until it eased then we trudged forwards again. I was worried that it would start icing soon. We'd have to give up the search if that happened. It was just too risky.

Out in the park it was a stygian night with no stars or moon, the wind howled through bare branches that rattled and swayed ominously. I thought longingly of home, a good book, and hot cocoa. I was glad for our halogen headlamps and hard hats from the van. I clipped red signal

lights to the dogs' coats, so they could be visually located; the night was now as black as their fur.

My girls weren't having much success, what with the wind and the time lapse. I walked a few paces away from the guys; Deep had now parked and joined us. I looked at the paths as they branched out. Which did you take, Mr. Walker?

An Alzheimer patient was usually "sticky." They'd go forward until there was something that stopped them. Of course, they also bounced into that something like a ping pong ball so it could be that he rerouted either right or left down one of these trails. I centered myself and called to him in my mind and got nothing but the image of a warm coat and the gibber-jabbering of the woman.

I went back over to the guys. "What do you think?" I asked.

"Don't know, Lexi. Maybe we should split up, Gator and I can take Beetle, and you and Blaze can take Bella, and we'll head out in different directions."

"That sounds like a plan."

It was cold in earnest. Bella sniffed around the trail using her odd kicking gait that she used when she wore her booties. It was a bit of comic relief to watch her go. But she wasn't coming up with anything helpful. We traced the first path start to finish and went back. We jogged the second path, trying to stay warm and make more progress. Nada. We were about to start the third possibility, when we heard the patter of ice hitting the sidewalk fast and hard.

"Shit." I looked up at the sky.

"It won't do Mr. Walker any good if we're not functioning. We may have to take a break — these trees'll become dangerous in short order." Blaze cupped his hands to yell over the baying wind. "We'll stay with it, though, as long as we can. I'll just call Iniquus and have them meet us with the—"

Before he could finish his sentence, sharp barks went up. Beetle! Beetle had a hit. That was her signal that she had found her target.

I had Bella's radio, so I couldn't follow a signal to the other team, and the wind made it hard to echo-navigate. I sent Bella out to lead us. Beetle would trumpet until I got there. Gator and Deep didn't know the signal for completion, "Finished!"

When I ran up to the scene, I was confused. Deep and Gator were trying to coax a woman out from under the bench, but she wasn't budging. I could hear sirens coming closer. Deep had called 911 as soon as they found the woman.

"Beetle, Finished! Good girl." I said to quiet her. Beetle ran over to me, overjoyed with her success. I scrubbed her fur to thank her. I took the backpack from Blaze, and got more heater packs out and opened. I stuck them all around the woman, and then I opened the silver emergency blanket. With Gator reaching under one side of the bench, and me reaching under the other, we tucked it around the woman who lay there wrapped tightly in a dark, wool, man's coat that looked fresh and clean, dichotomous to the woman herself.

Beetle and Bella came and sniffed at the cloth then lay down, a signal that they had a scent "hit" this was the smell that they had been searching for.

I kneeled down and put my face near hers so I could hear what this woman was saying.

"They're going to kill me. They know what I did to Johnathan St. James. I have to hide his body. I have to hide it now."

I lay down so we were face to face.

"They're going to kill me. They know what I did to Johnathan St. James. I have to hide his body. I have to hide it now," she repeated.

"Ma'am, can you tell me your name? Do you know where you are?" I asked, doing my EMT assessment to see if she was cogent. With her wild eyes and spittle at the corner of her mouth, she certainly didn't look sane.

"Ma'am, can you tell me your name? Do you know where you are?" she mimicked.

I scrunched my brow. "I drink lemonade on Saturday."

She repeated, "I drink lemonade on Saturday."

There was a crooked man, who walked a crooked mile, he found a crooked sixpence upon a crooked style. Huh. My psychic radar was definitely pinging now. I stood up and brushed myself off, as I caught movement at the top of the path.

The paramedics appeared with their gurney, and we signaled them over with our flashlights. They bent to coax and pull the woman out from under the bench, and I stepped to the side and called Missy.

Before Missy's midnight flight with her kids to the relative safety of DC after her husband's control snapped like dry kindling, she had worked in the Richmond psychiatric hospital, Tucker Pavilion.

"Missy, have you ever heard of a psych diagnosis which makes people parrot what they last heard?"

"Parrot, like a bird?"

"Repeat a last heard phrase?"

"Sure, it's called echolalia. That can happen in people on the autistic spectrum and also in schizophrenics. Why? Does this have something to do with the guy that went missing? I've never heard about instances of echolalia in people with Alzheimer's... But then again, that wasn't the population I worked with."

"No. This is someone else we came upon. We just need to get her some help. I've got to go. Thanks, Missy." I immediately hung up and called Dave. "Lexi here, it sounds busy where you are. Are you fighting the hoards for the last box of Twinkies at the convenience store?" I stuck my finger in my ear so I could hear him over the emergency responders and the woman yelling at the top of her lungs.

"I wish. I got called in to headquarters. It's all hands on deck for this storm. You, young lady should be home." His stern-father voice made me smile.

"Very soon. Can you check your data base for me? I need to know if there's a murder case about a man named Johnathan St. James."

"Give me a couple minutes, and I'll check. Does this have something to do with the missing case?"

"Maybe? Give me a call back asap either way, okay?"

"You got it."

The rescue team packaged the confused woman for the ride to the hospital and took off. It wasn't a night for pleasantries and small talk.

"Walker doesn't have a coat anymore." Blaze rested his hands on his hips. "He's going to die of hypothermia. I'd give him an hour tops."

"Let's let the ambulance head on down the road. With the coat scent gone, maybe the dogs can pick up another trail. From here on out we need to stick together, though. This weather... my eyes scanned the sky. "Each of you needs to decide whether you want to continue or not."

With an all-in from my teammates, I tasked Beetle and Bella to find the scent and offered them the pillow case once more. They moved in unison to the edge of the park headed down toward the Potomac. My phone buzzed against my frozen fingers, and I fumbled it to my ear.

"Lexi, Johnathan St. James is a Washington DC missing person case. He was a British national who disappeared here in DC August 28, 1959. No trace. Presumed dead. His wife said he had a gambling problem according to the notes. There's not much else in the file other than a photo."

"Walker was born in 1933 that would make him 26 when St. James disappeared."

"What's this about, Lexi? This is no time to be heating up a cold case."

"No, just trying to figure out where this guy could have gone. Thanks for your help, Dave. I'll check in later." I slipped my phone back into my jacket pocket. "Hey guys, let's think this through. According to lost person behavior, statistically, two things could be in play here. Because of the

severity of Mr. Walker's cognitive decline, I was going on the idea that he'd follow a single direction of travel. He'd get somewhere with a barricade, be it a building, a wall, a tree, and he'd ping-pong on that surface until someone found him."

"But now you're changing your mind?" Deep asked.

"Well, another scenario would be that Walker is oriented toward the past. That is, his mind is operating in a different year. So here's a stretch. What if Mr. Walker was oriented toward a different time period and was mumbling to himself. If his mind is not in the here and now, he could be operating in 1959, the year that Johnathan St. James from England went missing. Mr. Walker could have been mumbling about that, it was picked up and mimicked by whomever it was who was wearing Mr. Walker's coat, and now we're not only looking for an elderly man with dementia, we might also be on the trail of a killer."

Blaze was grinning. "Now this is why I like to go on adventure with you, Lexi. It always turns into some kind of shitstorm that keeps everything interesting."

"Speaking of shitstorms," Deep said, "we need to keep moving before we turn into popsicles."

That's when Beetle and Bella put their noses in the air and took off running.

Thank goodness I had their radio collars on them. Thank goodness there were no cars on the streets. The guys and I slipped and slid down the sidewalk, doubled over against the wind, glancing anxiously at the tree limbs that groaned above us. We climbed over a large oak already downed in the streets with strands of telephone wires tangled into its bare branches.

We were getting too far from the Humvee and too far to hoof it home. This search was everything that my rescue group taught us not to do. No one should ever take on this kind of risk. With the weighty sense of failure, I whistled for my dogs to come back to me. The wind carried the sharp note in the opposite direction.

I struggled to pull my dog whistle from the chain that hung between my breasts, keeping the metal warm under layers of outwear. Just as I put it to my lips, I heard the dogs bark victory. Even though we wanted to run in their direction, the best we could do was bend low and push against the wind.

By the time we got to them, Beetle and Bella had found a hollow in a wall and had climbed in like the smart girls that they were. Mr. Walker, dressed in his wool pants, a turtle neck, and a sweater, didn't look cold at all. He was actually sweating like his brain had convinced his body that it was a hot August night. He cussed under his breath and the clouds of his exhale carried the words up into the frigid air. He worked to move bricks from a dilapidated stair, that lead to an even more dilapidated house, into a pile.

Blaze got on his comms and got an all-weather extraction unit headed our way from Iniquus. We weren't going to bother 911. An ambulance didn't have the chains and armor to get an emergency team through this weather. Until support got to us, we let Walker stay warm by moving his bricks.

Two stories hit the news about Bruce Walker that week. One, his miraculous rescue carried out by citizens in the worst winter storm in recorded DC history. The second

was that he would not be charged with the murder of Johnathan St. James, though the missing man's skeleton had indeed been found under the pile of bricks that Mr. Walker was re-stacking.

For me, the whole episode was an affirmation that my psychic "knowings" were always accurate, even if they were impossible to decipher until I looked back at events in my rearview mirror. There was indeed a crooked man, who walked a crooked mile. At the site of the body the CSI found a crooked sixpence though it was *underneath* a crooked stile (of sorts). I will probably never know what it meant that "he bought a crooked cat who caught a crooked mouse," but those remains were all found together under the base of a very crooked house.

THIS IS NOT THE END

You can read more about Lexi and her adventures with her psychic twist in the LYNX series
and the soon to be released STRIKE FORCE series

© FIONA QUINN 2016. ALL RIGHTS RESERVED.

+++

3

SQUATTER

Ulla Håkanson

I jerked from a sound and looked up from my book. *What was that?* I nudged my husband sitting beside me on the sofa. "David, did you hear that?"

"What?"

"Shhh. Just listen..."

David put his book down and listened. "I don't hear anything."

"I heard a scratching sound. Here in the room somewhere..."

We both waited, listening.

"There it is again." I turned and looked back over my shoulder. "It sounds like an animal." I pulled my feet up on the sofa.

David's brow creased. "Where did that come from?"

"Over by the back wall, I think."

David put his book down and went to the back of the room. He put his ear to the wall and stiffened. "What the heck...?" He quickly crossed the room, went out the sliding door and into the backyard.

"Where are you going?" I got up and followed him.

David was squinting up at the wall. "There's a hole in the wall. A big one."

"Do you think it's a rat?"

"I think maybe a squirrel..."

"I read that squirrels nesting inside a house can chew through wires—which is a fire hazard. And if they get trapped in the house, they'll chew through window frames to get out."

"Maybe this one has tired of nuts."

"Don't just stand there and look," I said. "We'll have to do something. Why didn't it move in with our crazy neighbor who feeds them all the time?"

David looked over at their neighbors' house. "Could be that stucco isn't on the squirrel's menu."

"Well, I'm calling the SPCA," I said and left.

I looked them up on the web and called a nearby branch. A man advised me to rent a cage, place it on the ground beneath the hole and put a dab of peanut butter inside.

"Hopefully the squirrel living in your house will get trapped at some point," he said. "Then let it loose in a park, two to three kilometers away so it won't find its way back."

We rented a cage, put a generous spoonful of peanut butter inside and rigged it. The next morning, a squirrel was trapped inside.

I stared at the squirrel trying to push through the cage bars. "It looks frantic," I said. "And the cage-handle is very close to its teeth." I looked at David. "*You* take it."

David checked the time and shook his head. "I have to be downtown in forty minutes. Beth, please, you have until ten, and you're passing Sunnybrook Park."

"Okay... If you put it in my car."

"Sure."

I anxiously watched as David picked up the cage. He looked at me and frowned. "What is it?"

I smiled. "I just wanted to make sure..."

"I see." David nodded. "If the damn thing didn't eat my hand, you'd be fine. Is that it?" He looked at the squirrel. "What's the matter, Houdini? Waiting for a more tender cut?"

"Oh, all right. Give it to me." David held it until I had a secure grip of the handle.

When I reached the park, I realized it was only one kilometer from home, but decided that'd have to do. After pulling up to a grassy spot near the entrance trail, I opened the rear door and lowered the cage to the ground. Then I went around the car and slid across the back seat on my stomach. I reached over and pulled the cage door open, yelling, *"GO, GO, GO."*

The squirrel stood frozen for a second, then shot through the air like a rocket and disappeared into the park.

"Phew," I said out loud and slumped on the seat in relief.

I heard women's voices and hurried to put the cage in the trunk. I was about to get into the car, when my neighbor and a friend appeared between the trees.

My neighbor gave me a disapproving look.

"Some people think they can park anywhere they like," she said to her friend as they passed.

Old nag, I though, got in the car and drove to work.

"So how did it go today?" David said, back home from work. "You survived the battle with the beast I see." He grinned.

"Piece of cake," I lied, not wanting him to know that I'd been scared.

"Glad you feel that way." David said. "I'll rig the cage again before it gets dark. If we're lucky, we caught the one living in our house. We'll know by tomorrow."

The next morning there was another squirrel in the cage.

"Another piece of cake," David said. "Well, you know what to do," he added and left for work.

I called the SPCA again. "Try soaking a rag in ammonia and fill it with mothballs," said the man answering. "The big ones."

After dinner, I watched David make the stinking bundle and use a broom handle to push it as far into the opening as he could.

"That should be an easy choice," he said after adding peanut butter to the cage and rigging it. "Let's have a beer and watch the news."

Halfway through the evening news, a different sound from the wall had us both bolt out of our chairs. "Sounds like it picked the mothballs," I said as we hurried over to the wall to listen. It was a dragging sound this time, slowly moving in the direction of our cedar closet at the other end

of the room. A moment later, there was a thump, then silence.

"That little bugger is up to no good," David growled. "It shouldn't get peanut butter and a new home, it should..." He stopped when he saw my accusing stare. His frown changed to a forced smile. He pointed to the wall. "That little darling should be in heaven. Right, Honey?"

"Barbarian," I muttered. "I'm going to bed."

The smell woke us. David sat up and sniffed.
"Smells like mothballs."
"It's Saturday," I mumbled. "Go back to sleep."
"I can't sleep with this stink. I'm going to have a look."

We followed the smell, which was strongest near the cedar closet. As soon as we went inside, the fumes made our eyes water.

"God have mercy," David said as we scrambled to get out and slammed the door shut. He pointed to the room. "That's not a moth-safe room anymore, it's a *death* chamber."

"What kind of critter would drag that noxious heap all that way?" I wondered.

"A gourmet freak gone mad?" David guessed, rubbing his eyes.

I grabbed his arm. "David, I can't hear it anymore. Check the cage. Maybe it got sick of the smell and went out."

"Out for dinner?"
"Whatever."

"Nausea doesn't usually bring on a raving appetite, but hey, let's not jump to conclusions."

We looked outside. A new squirrel had gone for dinner.

"That's the one," I said. "I know it."

"I hope so," David muttered.

Later that morning, I moved the squirrel to the park.

Back from work, David plugged the hole with a large piece of wood. "Now, try to get into the house, you little bugger," he said, inspecting the wall. He slapped an extra layer of peanut butter on the cage floor, and rigged the cage.

The next morning, there was a new hole beside the plug and a new squirrel in the cage. This squirrel was missing its tail. It screeched at us in brazen indignation.

"This is *war*," David yelled.

As I brought the cage to my car, David went to his workshop. A moment later he came out with a large piece of chicken-wire. Curious, I followed him and watched as he nailed it over the hole with a hundred nails. *He's losing it.*

The old woman next door peeked through the hedge and asked if everything was all right. I told her we had problems with squirrels.

"Problems? How can you have problems with those friendly little things? They eat right out of my hand." She paused and looked thoughtful. "Although lately, there haven't been many around…"

David glared at her and was about to say something when I let out a faked laugh. "I was just kidding. My husband is fixing the wall."

"Oh?" The woman looked at the chicken-wire, then at David, then back at the chicken-wire. She shook her head, muttered something about shoddy workmanship, and left.

When the coast was clear, I transported the tailless critter to the park, wondering how many more times it would take before we caught the squatter.

That evening, David slapped a mound of peanut butter all over the cage floor, emptied a full bag of peanuts in the shell on top, and rigged it. He stood up and looked at it with his fists on his hips. "Sometimes I wish I had a gun," he muttered.

And that was it. The morning after, the cage was empty.

"*Greed* did it in," David laughed, grabbed my hands and danced around with me. "Only the best house and the most lavish buffet would do..."

We stiffened as the woman next door called out, "Oh, *there* you are, my little friend. Welcome back. Where have you been? Come get your breakfast." Lowering her voice as if it were a secret, she then said, "But Sweetness, you do know I can't feed you too much, don't you...?" As if understanding the old woman, the critter responded with teeth-chattering chirps and whistles.

David and I looked at each other in alarm. We edged closer to the hedge. There, up on its hind haunches was the squirrel with the lopped-off tail. Its

nose and whiskers twitched cheekily as it seemed to listen intently to what the old woman was saying.

We were too far away to hear what she said; but the woman was pointing in the direction of our house. On her perfectly manicured lawn led a trail of nuts straight for our hedge.

© Ulla Hakanson 2016. All rights reserved.

+++

4

NOTHING BUT THE TRUTH

Joseph Mark Brewer

I David's Parents

Well, your honor, it's like I said to that officer, I said: I knew David. I was his neighbor, you see. Knew his parents, too. Didn't know them, but met them. When they moved in. Can't really say I liked them. Didn't like what they did to old Mrs. Wilkerson's rose trellis, poor woman. Dies all alone. House emptied out by her family. I kept up the yard and the garden. Told the realtor I'd be glad to do it. It was the place next to mine, you see. Same plot. Only a little chicken wire fence between their yard and mine. Same lawn. I had an interest in keeping up the place.

It was autumn when they moved in, you know. School had already started. Poor David had to start school late. That matters when you're seven. Like I said, I can't say I really liked Helen or Marvin. They never really ever talked to me, you know. But I never saw them, really. Their side

door and their driveway was on the far side of their house, so I never saw their comings and goings. All I saw was the yard, which they neglected even after tearing down the rose trellis. And I saw through the windows. Ten feet from mine to theirs. Not much in the way of the front room, but plenty to see in the back. Kitchen and back porch and back yard. Funny how people live their lives in the back of the house.

You can tell a lot about people from how they keep up the back of their place. My back porch, iris bed, sidewalk, tomato patch, sidewalk to the garage—you could take a picture of it and put it in a magazine any time of the year. I don't mind saying that. Nothing was out of place. I liked it that way. I had to look at it, didn't I? Trim and tidy.

Not them, though. I could tell you about the windows. They were never washed, so you can imagine the dishes that piled up, day after day. I'd see the breakfast things setting on the table long after David left for school and Helen and Marvin went wherever they went off to. Never did find out what he did for a living. Helen said she was a beautician. Not that I'd know. Had no use for those places.

I didn't know Helen or Marvin well at all, you could say, but I knew David. He'd be by himself, playing in the yard. Kicking a ball. Digging in dirt. I could tell he had an imagination on him even back then. Some of the things he'd make with just some old cardboard boxes he'd pull from the garage. He'd walk home from school and never once step into the house. Straight to the garage to get whatever he was going to play with that afternoon while he waited for Helen to come home. She came home first, you see. Long about five thirty I'd see the back door open and

David would scamper onto the back porch and kick off his shoes and go inside. That was it.

I remember the first day David waved hello to me. He was playing in the yard and was just staring off into space like some kids do. I could tell he wasn't looking at the poplars in the corner of their yard or the sugar maple in the corner of mine, or the clouds either. I think he just noticed my house, like he was seeing it for the first time. Caused me a bit of a fright, you know, realizing his eyes were on mine all of a sudden. Well, he waved. Just like that. Not much of a smile, but he waved. And I guess I waved back. That must have satisfied him because he went back to his playing. I don't recall what I did the rest of the day. That boy had the saddest eyes I ever saw.

David's parents, well … I should say Marvin, his father, he was gone a lot. He'd be gone then show up and I'd see David in the yard playing with something or other. All the time they were there I never saw Marvin in the kitchen. It's like he didn't eat. Maybe he didn't. Not there. Helen sat at that cluttered table and drank coffee and smoked cigarettes and you can bet that after dinnertime the light was out and that was it 'til morning. And David was lucky to get a bowl of cornflakes for supper, I can tell you that.

I know it was like that for years, you see. No neighbors visited more than once. No relatives came by that I ever saw. No kids stopped by for trick or treat, but I don't see out the front all that much. It was a lonely life for them over there.

And then the day came when Marvin walked out the back door on to the porch and out to the driveway and I noticed the car parked there. I saw he had two suitcases and

he put them in the back seat and drove off. That was the end of Marvin.

It was summer, you know, when Marvin left, and that night I watched David in the back yard, like he did every night he could, catch lightning bugs. He'd catch them in a jar like kids do. I watched him tear the wings off and he'd write something in the sky, watching the fluorescent green make some kind of writing or another. I think I saw him spell his name. D-a-v-i-d. He was about 11 then.

II David

I said this to that other officer too: Helen began having male visitors, some of them those fellas you see at the Hitchin' Post or the Homestead or Hoppy's Garden, the shift workers from the paper plant, fellas who knew Helen as a woman with no man around and well, you know. I'm not one to judge. It just seemed awful to me, some Saturday morning Helen would sit and have coffee with a man whose name I can't tell you, and David would walk right past out the door and get on his bike and go anywhere but his own house. It's bad when you're twelve. It's worse when you're older.

David had a paper route by then and was up early in the morning delivering papers, and went out every week and collected. He'd have come to my house if I took the paper but I didn't. That's why I say I never ever spoke to him. Not ever then, with that paper route and him collecting every week. But I saw him, right at five every morning, out of the house, rain or shine, on his bike, out in the world.

If you ask me that's when he started acting like he was older than his years.

He never had any friends over, like I said. He went to school and came home and spent a long time in the garage. I think he liked to tinker. Build things. I'd see him through that garage window. His head would bob back and forth and then he'd turn on a light and that'd cast a shadow across the lawn. He'd walk in and out with one tool or another, and that spring out came a lawnmower I never saw before, on account of them having a spinning push mower. This had a one-horse-power Briggs and Stratton engine and he could start it up with one pull. I'd see him push it out of the garage and head down the alley and within minutes, I'd hear that engine roar for twenty minutes or so, and I just knew he was making pocket money.

No, he never came to me to ask to cut my yard. I think Helen told him more than once not to bother me. I don't know why, I'm no bother and it would have been good to have the company, but that's how it is, you know?

So like I said, I only saw him next door and in the kitchen window and in the garage. But I can tell you that was when he sprouted up the way kids do. Yes, I know you know I must know all about that, and that's not what I mean. He wasn't a little kid anymore is all I'm saying. I can tell you that just from gauging his height from the latch on the garage door. He must've shot up six inches that summer he was thirteen and mowing lawns and delivering papers.

Still, it was the same routine. Helen had some fella around for a week or two, and David made himself scarce as usual. I think school was relief for him, and then he got to that age he didn't come right home after school, either.

No, I don't know where he would go. I said I never leave the house.

So you want to hear about what happened? Ain't that what I been trying to tell you? Okay then. I seen his life and Helen's life and the way things were. Well, you know David had to be a smart kid. He reached the age where he could do things for himself. He'd come home from delivering papers and he'd be hungry so he just made his own breakfast. I know. I watched him. Made his own bacon and eggs. Made his own pancakes. Learned how to make his own biscuits in that gas oven. I know that from Mrs. Wilkerson herself. She was so proud when she bought it.

Anyway, he began making his own coffee too. And don't think Helen minded. She'd come down and help herself and light a cigarette and drink that coffee and never once did I ever see her say thank you. David did his own washing up, too. He never learned that from Helen either, I can tell you.

Helen. I think her drinking got worse. You can tell it in a woman just like a man, they let themselves go, their skin gets all splotchy. I don't blame her for drinking and Marvin was not much of anything to be proud of, but once he left her she went downhill fast. Walked around the house in her nightgown, a cigarette hanging out of her mouth. No fellas came around much after that. David was out the house as much as possible. I tell you, he'd have moved into the garage if it was possible.

Look, I know you know what happened, but that's what I'm trying to tell you. It was this way. Yes, it was a Sunday morning, and yes, David was out of the house

delivering papers. But I saw him turn on the stove. Helen was already sitting at the kitchen table from the night before, passed out. He fiddled with the stove before heading out the door to the garage. He was in there a few minutes before fetching his bike and pedaling away to do his paper route.

Then I saw Helen raise her head and sniff the air. I saw her. And I saw her drunk, confused look on her face as she reached for a cigarette and flicked her lighter. That's when the whole kitchen blew up.

Of course he left the gas on, and I can't say he did it on purpose. Kids are forgetful. But that garage went up too, not ten minutes after he left. Like a bomb. Just one big whoosh and everything sky high. No Helen. No house. No garage.

I always liked David. Nice boy. You watch 'em grow up and, well... You never know, do you?

No, your honor, I ain't seen David since. Not Sunday, not Monday, not today. And you ain't ever gonna see him again, I can tell you that.

© JOSEPH MARK BREWER 2016. ALL RIGHTS RESERVED.

+++

5

ANGEL HEART

Michelle Medhat

Faster, and faster she spun, and the world collapsed into a kaleidoscope of numbing colour and meaningless sound. All so beautiful. People were beautiful. Their faces she could see clear and distinct. So huge. So bright. Big bright, shiny faces. Laughing. And spinning, and spinning. Endlessly.

A dizziness tinged with euphoria swept over Jem. Such a feeling. She didn't want it to end.

Leaving the lounge, the party pounding into overdrive, Jem headed for the roof garden terrace. Kos, her boyfriend of the moment, dutifully followed.

A warm wind lashed softly against her cliff-high cheekbones; her supple young skin flushed dusky pink, and her emerald eyes sparkled with specks of narcotic-inspired glitter.

She had to admit, it'd been amazing. Jem had tasted incredible highs before, but none came close to what she felt now. She was, without doubt, in Elysium. Reaching out, arms wide, she grabbed hold of Kos. And it was all down to

him, the reason for this wonderful feeling.

Jem kissed him deep, tugging at his clothes, stripping him in seconds. Giggling, she dropped to her knees, showing her gratitude. Kos looked down, a smug sneer formed casting doubt on his outwardly angelic appearance. Seen it all, done it all. And still the bitches came. When would they ever learn.

Needing lubrication, he lunged at the Cristal, still giggling mischievously. Jem rose and snatched the bottle and tipped it above her head, meaning to gulp the drink down. But her coordination was way off. The champagne spilt down the right side of her mouth, down her chin, down her slender neck and slid slowly down her full cleavage. Kos stuck out his fat, pink tongue and lapped at the pool between her breasts, moving up he licked at her neck and sucked greedily at the champagne dripping like pale yellow pearls from her chiselled chin.

"Want some more...?" asked Kos, glaring expectantly at Jem.

Jem flopped down in her Philip Starck 'Ghost' chair, elbows on knees, face cupped in hands, she stared out across the city, her eyes plate-wide and glassy, flickered, momentarily lost. Then she caught the vibe again.

"Um ... yeah ... okay," slurred Jem, captivated by the twinkling lights of London's nightscape.

On the table, an assortment of tablets, phials and plastic pockets. Kos lent in and picked a little packet. A small, pink sequin heart was fused into the plastic. Kos smiled coldly. Lenny had style. His brand, 'Angel Heart,' was infamous, a real club brand. Always cut with just a little more jazz then the rest. Guaranteed to give an unpredictable punch.

He ripped open the top of the packet, tipped the contents on to a small solid silver platter, and split the cocaine into little silos with his Amex Black card.

"Hey gorgeous, try this..."

Kos balanced the platter on Jem's thin knees. In a daze, Jem took the rolled up £50 tube Kos handed to her, shoved it in her nose and snorted the ivory powder.

"Good girl, you like it? Come on, take some more..."

On the first hit, Jem felt light-headed and airy, but the world wasn't so well defined as before. The sharp, clear edges; the vivid, vibrant colour all seemed washed out, like someone had brushed it with water. Around her everything was fuzzy, grainy and not quite there. Maybe another hit, a real big hit, would get back perspective.

Jem dropped her head and snorted hard the 3-inch silo in one go. Kos was impressed. Glancing over his shoulder to the lounge where inside, Lenny was busy pleasuring the underage daughter of a cabinet minister and a rock star's daughter simultaneously, Kos made a surreptitious thumbs up. The signal told Lenny they had snared another source of profit.

Surging through her nasal passage, the second hit impacted. Jem's chest tightened, she gasped for air, panicking, and inhaled quickly. She didn't know what was happening. On entering her bloodstream, the first hit attacked her pancreas. By the second hit, her pancreas was already ejecting lethal protein enzymes. These enzymes headed straight for her lungs, damaging the tissue; filling the small air sacs and capillaries with blood and fluid and restricting the movement of oxygen from inhaled air into the blood. As the air sacs filled, less oxygen could get

through, Jem's breathing became more rapid and shallow.

"Help me!"

Awash with lethargy, Jem slipped back into the chair, the platter tumbled to the floor, clattering loudly on the terracotta tiles.

Kos turned at the sound back to Jem. Low oxygen in her blood had turned her full, soft red lips powder blue and mottled her delicate, young skin. Unable to breath, Jem's hands clawed at her throat, confused and bloodshot eyes flicked back and forth, searching for "why this was happening to her."

"Oh Shit!"

Kos just stared at Jem's throes of respiratory arrest, not moving. That's just fucking great! Now he'd have to find another rich kid to meet his monthly quota…

Other people at the party had heard Jem's cries and drifted to the terrace.

"Hey, she must've had some bad shit," said a skinny blonde in a belt for a skirt and an edible string bead bra (half eaten).

"Man, you don't need that …," said a guy with a buzz cut, fishnet sequin vest and black leather thong.

Kos knew he was right; he didn't need it. Throwing his arms up in the air, he yelled: "Party's over…everyone out."

Stoned, sweaty semi-clothed party creatures grabbed at their Gina shoes and Chloe bags and scrambled out. Kos was sure they couldn't have moved faster if the floor had been alight with flames.

Lenny pulled up his jeans swiftly and pushed through the molten mass of bodies to get to the entrance. Like everyone else, Lenny just wanted to "get the hell outta there."

Kos looked round at the penthouse. They'd trashed it completely. Food and drink ground into the deep pile Axminster, used condoms strewn like trophies on the sofas and chairs; powders, pills and empty bottles collided making a psychedelic clash of colour on the lemon carpet.

Oh well, it was *her* place. And somebody else's problem, thought Kos closing the door.

+

Two days later, DCI Sarah Steiner stood amongst the party fall out, looked to the terrace and acknowledged her "new problem." Jemimah de Laine, daughter of the world-renowned scientist Sir Patrick de Laine, decomposing disgracefully in the sweltering summer heat.

"Here we go," she thought, snapping on her mandatory latex gloves. "Another day at the funhouse!"

Something about that corridor to the Path Lab. Dark; depressing. Ominous atoms clogged up the atmosphere, and always made DCI Steiner shudder. Police training should have eradicated supernatural thoughts and superstitions, but in that corridor Sarah could almost feel spirit fingers, wispy tendrils of the dead reaching out, touching her, imploring her to find their killers.

At certain times, when the cases were piled high and no resolution in sight, she imagined the victims clustered around her, hot holidaymakers around an ice cream stand begging for attention, eternally longing for her to right the wrong done to them.

But she wasn't a miracle maker, she could only work on facts, work on evidence, and use the only power God

bestowed on her: brain power.

Sarah shook away her plaguing thoughts of paranormal persuasion and pushed on the double doors. They swung in allowing her passage to the Path Lab. Stepping across the threshold, formaldehyde, ammonia and copper smells invaded her senses.

A stocky, short man in his mid-forties busied himself around a metal table. The man was Chief Pathologist Nigel Tavistock. He plunged his hands into the open cadaver and extracted the lungs. Sarah swallowed hard and looked away. She'd seen it before, so she wasn't queasy, but watching as the life of a pretty seventeen-year-old was reduced to a few organs, blood and body fluid, made her soul ache.

Staring into Jemimah's face, her stunning emerald eyes, now closed forever, Sarah struggled to comprehend how an intelligent, wealthy girl who had everything to live for could end up on an ice cold, marble slab.

"The lungs are full of fluid. See here..."

Tavistock pointed at the lower curve of the right lung. "This is where the enzymes started to break down tissue. I've run tests on the pancreas. It would've been kicking out poisonous enzymes 60 ml per every 100 ml of blood. At that rate her lungs wouldn't have stood a chance."

"So this was an overdose?"

Sarah pushed back her shoulder-length brunette hair over her small, gently-rounded ear and moved closer to examine the lungs with Tavistock. Those who did not know Sarah could almost imagine her still at College. Small petite frame, pointy pixie-like face; a ray of innocence around her and at times, even teenage clumsiness, but all these features combined to form a powerful masquerade. The truth: Sarah

Steiner was no pushover, and at 28, although very young for DCI, she'd amassed a significant case book of solved crimes, and could boast experiences other officers of her rank could only dream of.

Leaving College prematurely, Sarah had drifted, never quite finding that job to make a difference. Just by sheer chance, she'd been on a bus going through Canary Wharf. A girl got on at Canada Water, all City pin-stripes and sensible Chanel handbag and shoes. The girl appeared uneasy. Sarah watched her intently and a weird, twisted feeling erupted inside her gut.

The girl dove in her bag and tried to fiddle with something. Careful not to attract the girl's attention, Sarah peered inside. Instead of usual girly things like make-up bags and purses, Sarah saw metal and wires. Before Sarah recognised what she was doing, her instincts took over. She leapt on the girl, pulling her hands from the bag. Happening so unexpectedly, the girl had no time to react, Sarah's fist delivered a heavy blow to the girl's temple and she fell. Sarah screamed out, "She's got a bomb!"

That day Sarah saved lives. She was nominated for a bravery award, and although her courageous, if albeit insane action was commended, the Prime Minister made a speech stating that 'perhaps jumping on one's fellow passengers was not the most appropriate of actions to take and these had been extreme circumstances.'

A career in the police force beckoned soon after. And her life blossomed as Sarah found new meaning to her life. She saved lives. That was what she was good at. And that was why she was saddened to see lives like Jem's lost.

"It's not just an overdose," replied Tavistock, picking

up a file. "The tox screen showed she had mescaline, amyl nitrate and sodium sulphate in her blood."

"Washing powder!" said Sarah, nodding.

"Yeah...that's right."

"It figures, some unscrupulous suppliers use other agents to pad out the volume and push up profit. It's either washing powder or baking powder. They're the favourites."

Sarah stared at the body, considering options: "Could be an allergic reaction, maybe anaphylactic shock?"

"No evidence of any anaphylaxis. But from the crystals found in her nasal passage she must have ingested a significant quantity all at once."

"Probably trying to impress," said Sarah, "I know I'd like to impress my bloody fist on the bastard that gave her that stuff."

Tavistock swung round, his face plainly displaying disapproval at the undisciplined outburst. Sarah didn't care. Yes, she was emotional. Yes, she was crazy. But did she get results? Yes, she bloody well did.

"SOCO brought in the forensics, we've run the semen and hair samples through the DNA database, and came up with this." Tavistock handed the sheet to Sarah.

"Lenny Barlow, now there's a surprise. GBH, extortion, rape, prostitution. What the hell was a nice girl like this..."

"...Doing with a bloke like that!" Tavistock finished the sentence, smiling, clearly showing that his humour hadn't been surgically removed when he became a pathologist.

"So Lenny's now into snowfake?"

"We don't know that. We don't know where she got it

from," cautioned Tavistock, one DNA scan did not a suspect make.

"I know that, but I think a little tête-à-tête with Lenny will prove rewarding," said Sarah, mentally noting his current address. "Call me if anything comes up."

At that, Sarah disappeared through the double doors.

Forty-five minutes later Sarah was pounding on Lenny's front door.

"What you want?" a young girl barely thirteen answered, her street-inspired arrogance whipped up around her.

"Lenny Barlow, where is he?"

"You want stuff?" The kid eyed Sarah in her t-shirt, hoody and hipster jeans. No way was she a copper, too small, too young, and way too cool.

"What you got?" replied Sarah playing along.

"I got it all. What you want?"

"Popular shit. Stuff that sells."

"You want Angel Heart," said the kid, falling back into the hallway. Sarah followed. No warrant, but "what the hell..."

"Here, it's cool!" The kid shoved a little packet with pink heart in front of Sarah's face. Sarah took the flimsy package. It looked harmless. The sequin heart gave the impression of cute and friendly, something you'd buy in Accessorize. Cocaine had gone mainstream, marketed as a fashion "must have." And the packaging was out to attract impressionable youngsters. Sarah felt sickened.

"How much," asked Sarah, keeping her thoughts focussed.

"50."

"Where's Lenny?" Sarah pressed again.

"He'd gone. Abroad on business, I think. So, you got cash?"

Sarah handed the money over. She should really take the kid into Social Services, not buy drugs off her. Overcome with worry for the kid's wellbeing, Sarah lapsed a moment in her cover, as she muttered: "So where's your parents?"

She may as well have said, "Hello I'm DCI Steiner." The effect would have been the same. Sarah realised her mistake, and reached out but the kid twisted, skilful precision borne out of experience, and slipped from her grasp. Pocketing the cash as she went, the kid sprinted across the lawn and down the road like a leopard had taken possession of her legs.

Sarah chased after the girl but she'd got a clear start, and the distance was widening.

"Put a watch on all the ports, airports and the Channel Tunnel for Lenny Barlow."

That bastard wasn't going to leave the country, thought Sarah, picking up new wind to save the girl from her own self.

Unfortunately for Sarah, Lenny already had.

+

A year later, Lenny Barlow, under his new moniker, Paul Noche, flew into a tiny private airfield in White Waltham in Berkshire. Within a week, he was back to his old tricks.

"Fuck man, you want ten keys, five don't do justice, ya know."

Lenny was in mid-flow, convincing Bobby, a new dealer, to take on more Angel Heart. The little shit only

wanted 5K and he had to off load 10K before the end of the week, otherwise Sergei would make a new coat out of his skin.

When Lenny had first heard of the practice, he believed it was drug folklore. Till he saw it with his own eyes. Sergei actually had garments made from the skin he'd flailed off of idiots stupid enough to think they could screw him. He wasn't going to end up in the wardrobe of that Ruskie pervert.

"Man, this stuff, you'll hit max, no question. Ten keys, you'll want more. Fuck! I know." Lenny tried to mask the motivation of desperation in his voice.

"Yeah, but my path isn't set yet. Ya know, my lines, got ta get my lines up, then I'll up it," explained the new dealer.

"Lines ain't no problem. They'll be queuing man, this stuff flies, fuck man, it's sweet, ya know. They'll want it."

"I dunno, ten Keys, time to shift. Want payback quick, man, can't wait, got commitments."

Lenny knew his persuasion wasn't working. Time to get tribal, that always worked.

"Bobby, if you yellow, ain't got the bottle, that's cool. I know Jess'll take what I'm offering. He's a real man, born winner, ya know."

"Hey, hey, I'm not saying I'm not buying, just saying shifting, gonna take time."

"So you buying." Lenny confirmed. He stared at Bobby and hid fear of rejection in his eyes with a cheerful glimmer. Simple trick to do, he just imagined a gorgeous bird doing the bizzo on him.

"Umm..." Still hesitation.

"Man, I gonna call Jess, he won't worry about shit like timescales. I gave you first off, 'cause you're new, wanted to give you an edge, but you're not jiving, that's cool. Jess'll buy, he knows good stuff..."

"Wait...no! I'll buy!"

"Ten Keys?"

"Yeah, full ten."

"My man, you're a star. You won't be disappointed. Girls love this, like nectar, you ... my man be the bee, ya know. It's sweet. You be 'heading' for heaven. Fast track, know man!"

"Know it, right." Bobby licked his lips at the thought.

Inwardly, Lenny breathed again. There was no Jess, of course. Bobby was the last chance to shift his load.

"At D, okay?" Lenny kept the talk to a minimum, and used dealer code to confirm on details. "At D" meant the meet would take place at the nightclub, Decadence.

"Yeah right."

"Ninety DL," code speak for 9 p.m.

"Cool."

"And sing, right?" Lenny wanted cash only.

"Yeah right sing, no problem."

"Century, no messing." £100,000 was the target Lenny wanted.

"Only do a Joe." Bobby could only stump up £90,000.

"Century man, this is real good. You'll shift and double no problem."

"Okay, okay...a Century."

"Bobby, my man, you be sweet. Later."

Lenny rang off, satisfied he'd tucked Bobby tight, and most of all, kept Sergei off his back, literally.

Boarding a train at Wandsworth, Lenny scanned the compartment, looking for talent. His seductive sapphire blue eyes and sculptured, toned body made him a babe-magnet. One flash of his full-on smile and the skinny chicks fell at his feet.

A Chinese girl, prim and quiet, nose in a book, didn't pay him any attention. Not my type anyway, Lenny mused, flicking a sideways swipe at other passengers. A bloke in running gear stank of sweat. No thank you. A petite, blonde at the end of the compartment caught his eye. Slim hips barely holding up the skin-tight jeans, a T-shirt two sizes too small displayed a taut tanned stomach adorned with a diamond droplet. Now that was his type. He moved in.

"Hi..."

The girl smiled shyly. "Hi."

"Going up West?"

"Yeah, Piccadilly, doing some shopping."

"Cool. I love shopping."

"You do?" The girl didn't believe Lenny. No guys she knew liked shopping.

"Oh yeah, I love it. I like to try before I buy. You like to try?" Lenny stared straight into the girl's hazel eyes, and very slowly, sided up closer to her.

"Yeah, I like to try. I do a lot of trying."

"Me too," Lenny noticed the girl had shifted her body weight forward, pressing out her breasts, her Malteser-sized nipples straining against the cotton-lycra mix.

"What d'ya do?" Lenny guessed being on a train at 11 o'clock on Monday morning, she was: 1) on her day off, 2) unemployed, or 3) rich with nothing to do. In his

experience, it was always one of these options, and Lenny hoped it was the last one.

The girl flushed embarrassed and looked away. "I don't do anything."

"You looking for work?"

The girl stared ahead, caught in a moment known only to her. Lenny thought he'd blown it. Thought he'd moved too quickly. Then she spoke.

"No, I don't do anything, I don't need to. My parents...um...they left me..." She halted, suddenly aware she was talking to a complete stranger. "It doesn't matter." She looked away again, hiding the tears transported by memories.

"I like to shop, that's it!" said the girl finally.

"That's cool. Nothing wrong with shopping," said Lenny gently, pretending to understand. She was beautiful, disturbed and rich. Handed to him, God, his life was charmed.

Lenny opened his mouth to advance his predictable patter but none came. Tremendous heat built in his body, and his heart somehow had started a marathon run without telling him. He could actually feel it thundering out of control. Tearing at his shirt, he grimaced in excruciating pain. He tried to scream but his voice couldn't muster strength.

A real catch to a shaking wreck in seconds, the girl watched horrified. Lenny reached out and grabbed hold of her t-shirt, but the fabric slid out of his sweaty hands and he fell. On the floor, he gasped and struggled for understanding as his heart ignored his internal rhythm and skipped cruelly out of sync.

"He seemed such a great guy," were the last words he heard before Lucifer wrapped his long, flaming tail around him and hauled him down to hell.

+

"Do you have a cause of death yet?"

Sarah looked on Lenny's body, ripped apart like a piece of prime beef, with impassionate eyes.

"From the state of his heart, it looks like atrial fibrillation," replied Tavistock.

"What brought that on?" Sarah knew atrial fibrillation was caused when the heart suffered a massive flux, changing its rhythm and internal beat.

"Ironically, tox screen showed up nothing. A dealer who didn't take."

"It happens. They're in it for the money not the high. Any ideas what caused the AF, if it's not drugs?"

"An electrical surge would do it. I've seen microwaves used to produce atrial fibrillation, that's a favourite of Russian drug lords. Microwave burns to a crisp but there are no burn marks on his body."

"So, what's your theory?" Sarah felt all she was doing was asking questions, Tavistock just wasn't forthcoming on answers. She was getting irritated. "You must have some idea?"

"I don't want to say this early but the post mortem's showing all the signs of natural causes.

Sarah wasn't buying it, a bloke like Lenny just didn't die naturally. She skimmed the SOC report. The principal witness was a girl. She confirmed he'd been acting totally

normal, when he suddenly grasped his chest and fell. She claimed that she neither saw nor heard anything. Other passengers corroborated the sequence of events of Lenny's demise. Tavistock was right, everything did point to a death by natural causes.

"Steiner, I think this one's a closed book."

"You think?"

"Accept it, Steiner, it was his time to go. Maybe God's revenge, who knows, but there's nothing suspect. Death by natural causes. Simple as that."

"Nothing's ever that simple..."

"Well, for me it is," said Tavistock cleaning his hands. "And unlike you, I have someone who needs me!"

Tavistock said his brusque goodbye and walked out of the path lab leaving Sarah alone with her memories. On the slab, Lenny's body had vanished, Jem de Laine's naked body sprawled across the marble. Sarah lent in. Jem's eyes flicked open and her arms stretched out towards Sarah, "Find them!"

Sarah blinked back terrified and Jem was gone.

And I have someone who needs me too.

+

"In some cases naturally occurring infrasound could produce feelings of fright, unease and even cold. Infrasound has been regarded as one of the most likely causes of supernatural phenomena such as haunted houses."

Sarah just happened on the article in a science magazine. It wasn't her usual read, but she was attracted by the front cover, a piece on 22nd century humans, and

anyway, her train had just been delayed.

Reading the infrasound article to the end, Sarah breathed in sharply on seeing the author's name.

Professor Sir Patrick de Laine, Chief Scientific Advisor, Cabinet Office

It had been a year since his daughter's death and two days since Lenny Barlow's demise. Jem's death had been attributed to respiratory arrest brought on by a massive cocaine overdose. The verdict had been death by misadventure. Her death had not been regarded as murder. Her party-girl profile suggested she took the drug by her own volition.

Sarah doubted that any force had been used. Certainly not physical, psychological was another story. Raising the bar higher, pushing Jem to take more would have been Lenny's modus operandi, but he would have done it with devious aplomb, so she wouldn't have noticed. All she would known was that she was having a "good time."

If she could've got to Lenny before he bolted, maybe a case of manslaughter might have stuck. But with his barrage of slick lawyers and a dearth of reliable witnesses, Sarah was cynically aware the case would have gone as far as an 80-year-old granny with a Zimmer frame in the London Marathon.

In cases of drug abuse, often the only people to blame were the parents. Sarah would never forget the moment she broke the news to Jem's father. She'd never seen anyone implode before.

Sir Patrick sat there in his majestic, high-ceilinged morning room and looked past Sarah into space. He didn't react. Didn't speak. Didn't move.

Sarah wondered whether he'd actually heard what

she'd said. Should she repeat it? Would he be offended if she did? She shuffled awkwardly and waited for a sign of recognition to the news she'd delivered.

Staring ahead, Sir Patrick's gaze fixed on something beyond human sight. Sarah noticed he didn't blink. Eyes huge, like they were propped open by invisible matches. Minutes passed, but Sir Patrick kept his concrete stare on the space beyond her chair.

Sarah knew something was very wrong.

"Sir Patrick, are you all right?" No response.

"Sir Patrick, are you all right?" Sarah repeated. Nothing. Only his cold, focussed stare fused to somewhere else.

"Sir Patrick," shouted Sarah loudly and she rose off the sofa and shook the scientist gently by the shoulders. Like shaking a tree trunk, he was solid and inert.

Sarah slid her finger across her phone to call the paramedics, but she'd barely given her call sign, when Sir Patrick spoke:

"I understand. Thank you for telling me. Now will you please leave. I wish to be alone." His voice was calm and pronounced. No sign of emotion. No flicker of pain.

Sarah slid her phone shut and scrutinised the man in front of her. His back was straight, his posture composed. He didn't look like a man who'd just been told his daughter had died. His attention was on her, and suddenly he was standing, his arm pointing the way to the door.

"Are you all right?" asked Sarah again, confused and amazed by his emotional turnaround.

"Yes thank you." His voice was clipped with an icy insistence. "Please go!"

Sarah moved towards the hallway, then turned back to face Sir Patrick:

"You'll want to see the body"

"No!" Sir Patrick emitted the instant response, but it sounded for a second like a painful growl of an injured animal.

Sarah was surprised—parents always wanted to see the body of their loved ones. It was a way to confirm that they were really dead and the police hadn't made a terrible mistake. But most of all it was to allow their final goodbyes to be said.

"Well maybe not now, obviously, but later when you've..." Sarah's words caught like a large olive pip in her mouth. Sir Patrick's face was alabaster. He looked like he'd suffered exsanguination by an unseen hand. His skin was baking-paper thin; his eyes, just vacant burrows. He barely looked alive. Only a head that shook with inherent determination indicated he was still breathing.

"No, no thank you, that won't be necessary."

"I really think..."

"Look, I don't want to be rude, but I'd really like you to leave, NOW!" Sir Patrick swept his arm in an arc ending in the direction of the front door.

Sarah stepped forward in silence, past Sir Patrick's outstretched arm, pointing like a sundial, and left without a further word of encouragement. *Well, I suppose people handle grief differently.*

She'd barely arrived back at her desk when the report came in:

"Disturbance at 189 Fulham Palace Road, two men fighting, dark haired male in mid-twenties and tall

Caucasian male in his fifties. Officers required to attend."

"Shit! That's Kostas Passellides' address. He was Jem de Laine's boyfriend!" Sarah called out to her Assistant DI. "Do you think someone's taking the law into their own hands?"

Arriving at the scene, Sarah saw what she'd expected in the drive over. Sir Patrick de Laine, the upright, noble and eminent cabinet scientist beating the living crap out of Jem's Greek God. On every remorse-fuelled kick, with tears dripping down his shattered face, Sir Patrick screamed his sorrow-filled mantra:

"You killed my baby ... you killed my baby!"

Wound up in his own retribution, Sir Patrick was oblivious to the Police's arrival. Limpet-like, he stuck to Kos, punching and kicking with a ferocity that actually scared him. It showed him just how barbaric humans could be...when pushed too far. It took two officers to prise him away from the bleeding, shaking mass. If they'd been any later, he knew he would have killed Kos.

Sir Patrick stared ahead, not facing Sarah. That same dead stare she'd witnessed earlier. A once great man who now had nothing left to live for.

Despite mitigating circumstances and a heavyweight lawyer, the judge, a mean old swine, sentenced Sir Patrick to six months' custodial sentence at Wandsworth Prison. He added he "wanted to make an example of Sir Patrick, sending a message that in matters of violence, such as the grievous bodily harm committed by Sir Patrick de Laine, class and status had no place. Everyone should be treated with equal contempt for engaging in such heinous crimes."

Sir Patrick shouted from the dock: "What about justice for my daughter? Where is the sentence for her killers?"

Hearing Sir Patrick's vitriolic invective, Sarah looked down, ashamed. She'd failed and a man had lost his honour through his desire for justice for the one he loved.

Before the officers turned him away, Sir Patrick delivered his last words straight to Sarah: "I will never forget what they did to her. I'll never stop searching for the truth ... even if you have."

Jarring back from her anguished recall to reality, Sarah stared again at the magazine article. If the tox screen had showed up nothing and no puncture marks were found on Lenny's body, an external influence must have been involved.

She couldn't do this on her own. She had a strong hunch but she needed someone to discuss it with, to bounce ideas off, and most of all, someone who had the knowledge to validate whether her hunch was scientifically viable or just plain crazy.

Scrolling through her contacts on her phone, she found Richard Blake. He'd left CID to explore his career at Defence Science and Technology Laboratory. He'd be the perfect person as a sounding board. She clicked on his number.

"Richard, hi, it's Sarah ... Sarah Steiner. Yeah I know, long time no speak, and all that ... Have you got time for a coffee? I've got something I'd like to pick your brains on ..."

+

Stare at people, that's what she liked to do. A multitude could be learned in one glance. With her head pushed hard against the window, Sarah sipped her gin and

tonic and took in the action that was Fulham Broadway. The evening rush hour produced all types from both sides of the social spectrum. A heaving, homogenous undulation of tired, sticky bodies streamed in and out the tube entrance. From her vantage point, she observed, feeling not quite one of them, as if her elevated position, somehow took her outside of all that which was below her.

Staring at the people: the girl crossing the road in her-up-to-the second trendy clothes; the city slicker climbing into his Beemer; the uptight 40-something looking at the gang of youths progressing down the street towards her; the young, shy guy with his first love; the yummy-mummy with her Conran push chair and designer twins; the rucksack carrying office worker tucking into his much-longed for sandwich; the loner, hands deep in pockets, kicking the ground; the elderly couple looking in bewilderment around them. Sarah wondered how many would turn into criminals. And how many would become killers?

She couldn't read minds. She couldn't look down and say that one person would be more likely to commit a crime than another. Oh, the sociologists would claim you could. Spouting their usual diatribe "of the environment makes the person," but Sarah didn't believe it. She believed, when pushed, a person could do anything, no matter of colour, creed, education or social status. When we're pushed too far, everything comes down.

"Hi."

Sarah looked up and instantly those Millennium lyrics *"all the best women are married all the handsome men are gay...you feel deprived"* sounded in her mind. God, she felt deprived, all right. Richard was a stunner. One of those guys

that women, whatever their taste, their preference were instinctively drawn to. But Richard Blake was in a class above preference. One date with him ... unfortunately, Richard's dream date was more David Cameron than Cameron Diaz.

Such a waste, thought Sarah, eyeing Richard with wistful longing, as he sat down conspiratorially close to her. His trademark 'Polo' lingering like an aura around him. Sarah flushed, after all the years they'd worked together she should be immune to the 'Blake Bombshell' effect, but like a dozy school girl with a crush on her science teacher, Sarah had fallen headfirst into his sparkling smile and dancing, dangerous dark brown eyes.

"What's been happening?" Richard asked as he moved his arm up around Sarah. Her heart somersaulted at his touch. Get a grip ... it's only friendship. She'd learnt a long time ago that Richard liked to be tactile with friends around him. He enjoyed the closeness of women and the intimacy of good old gossip. And that was where the line was drawn.

"Oh, nothing much," breathed Sarah.

"That so! Last I heard you'd made DCI. Bit young for that. Aren't you?"

"The Board didn't think so."

"Youngest DCI ever, apparently. Must have had the right mentor." Richard smiled.

"You would know." started Sarah, and then she realised that as nice as the banter was, she had work to do. "That's why I've asked you here, need to run a theory past you and I'd like you to validate its scientific viability."

"I'll have a go, tell me." Richard moved forward, showing interest.

"A young drug dealer died of atrial fibrillation. There was no puncture or burn marks, and no evidence of ingested substances, but his heart showed signs of a massive variation on the heart's beat, causing sudden strain and myocardial collapse."

"So far, sounds like natural causes."

"That's what the Coroner's gunning for, but I'm not sure."

"What make's you think otherwise, Sarah? Seems like a closed case."

"Something I read, an article in one of those popular science mags."

"Popular and science are words not normally found in the same sentence." Richard grinned ruefully. Sarah had forgotten his crusade to make science top of the UK agenda again.

"Yeah, well, I think maybe sound had something to do with this guy's death. Do you think sound could affect the heart?"

"Yeah, of course sound could affect the heart. But the sound you're talking about is low frequency infrasound. The level of harm depends upon the pitch or cycle, as the cycles decrease the deadlier the effects on the body."

"So what cycle would be needed to kill someone?"

"Let me explain a little about infrasound. At one hundred hertz, nausea, giddiness and even extreme fatigue sets in; at sixty to seventy-three hertz the body suffers from a temporary inability to breathe, headaches, and abdominal pain; at forty-three to seventy-three hertz signs of spatial orientation distortion and poor muscular coordination will occur. The most dangerous cycle is between one-to-ten hertz range, as it's alleged in the medical fraternity that seven

hertz is the resonant frequency of the body's organs, hence organ failure and death could occur during the broadcast of this frequency. Infrasound's been used by the military for decades. In World War II, Nazi propaganda engineers used infrasound to stir up anger in the large crowds that had gathered to hear Hitler. The result was a nation filled with anger and hatred. Nowadays, infrasound is used in war zones to unnerve the opposition. Broadcasts cycled at eighty to ninety hertz delivers nausea, disorientation and affects the human bowel ... in a well, rather negative way, hence the term "shit scared." Not very nice, but a vital part of psychological warfare. Every bit as important as weapons in a war situation."

"Yeah, yeah okay, that's fascinating." Richard was a mine of fabulous information, but sometimes he didn't know where to stop. Sarah had to focus his mind on the issues at hand. "But could this infrasound cause atrial fibrillation?"

"Sound waves are energy, no different to the waves in your microwave, or those waves coming from the sun. And if energy is applied in the wrong way, of course it's dangerous."

"But could it be used to kill someone?"

"In theory, a low frequency cycle could be used to create rhythmic dysfunction in the heart. But we're walking into fantasy-land Sarah. The energy source needed to generate such waves would need to be huge. I suppose, though, if you kept it in a building, maybe next door to where the guy died."

Sarah shook her head: "No, no, he died on a train, at Wandsworth station."

"Other passengers around?"

Sarah nodded.

"No way, Sarah, it's impossible. People around raises the number of variables—places where errors could potentially occur. It just wouldn't..."

Richard stopped speaking, his face pensive, thoughtful: "Unless your assailant used a tag that would enable the sound waves to be targeted directly to the victim."

"What kind of tag?"

"Oh, Sarah, you know, just a straightforward radio frequency identification tag. Receiving signal only, so it could be really small."

"What would it look like?"

"Small, like a microdot, so it wouldn't be noticed on the victim's body."

"So it could be done..." Sarah could detect excitement building. Her theory was gaining credibility faster than red cards at Italy/England not-so-friendly football match.

"But Sarah, that doesn't change the fact you'd need an energy source of a significant size."

"Could this energy source be portable?"

Richard shot a gauche glance at Sarah, and turned away. He didn't want to face Sarah for fear he'd be read.

"It could be, if someone found a way to compact the power supply, but current research doesn't hold much hope of that happening any time soon."

Sarah listened and dejection splat on top of her like heavy raindrops, and her enthusiasm and optimism was soaked through.

"Sod it; I thought I was on to something. But from what you've said, it's just pie-in-the-sky theories. Back to the

drawing board."

Taking a long sip of her drink, Sarah was aware of a sudden atmosphere that had erupted between them. Uncomfortable silence had snatched away at their previous animated deliveries.

Sarah watched Richard shut down. His face contemplative, as if he was weighing up pros and cons on an unknown decision. His face tightened; a sigh rippled through him signifying he'd come to a decision. He learned forward and pulled Sarah close to him, whispering in her ear.

"Can I be sure of your confidentiality?"

"What!" Sarah responded taken aback. She was quite frankly hurt by Richard's suggestion that she could ever be indiscrete.

"Look, your theory, well, it has potential. Don't scrap it."

Sarah's eyes opened wide in utter disbelieve. No different a response as if Richard had confirmed the existence of aliens and, by the way, they really liked sci-fi TV. Sarah turned fully toward Richard to study him.

"What the hell does that mean? What do you know about all this?" Sarah wasn't going to let go. If Richard was concealing something, hiding vital information, perhaps even obstructing her investigation, she would get to the truth.

"Richard, you *must* tell me what you know?" Sarah demanded; her cold, interrogative stare fixed hard on her ex-CID friend.

"Not sure if I can." He looked down and examined his immaculate, manicured fingers.

"Richard, for Christ's sake, this is a murder investigation. You're prejudicing my enquiries."

Richard stared at the floor; then out the window, shrugged, seemingly reconciling his earlier decision that Sarah could keep a secret, and then finally spoke: "Our team have been working on an infrasound energy device. Portable. Ideal for certain military applications, like sieges. It's top secret, I shouldn't be telling you. I'll lose my job if this gets out."

"It won't; don't worry."

Richard half smiled, but then his worried face overrode the initial sentiment. He'd been treading a fine line, and now he was aware he'd just jumped a foot on the wrong side.

"Richard, you can be assured of my discretion." Richard nodded, grateful, but still not convinced her word would hold, once the investigative process took over.

Sarah returned his nod, wondering what on earth Richard was about to reveal.

"What kind of size are we talking about for the device?" Sarah pressed harder.

A quizzical grin flitted across Richard's face. "You know those shopping trolleys that old ladies run around with? Well, that's it."

"What! A shopping trolley!"

"Yeah, it was perfect for the prototype, portable and easy to hide."

The CCTV image from the tube exploded into Sarah's mind with breath-taking clarity.

"Richard, sorry, I've got to go. Thanks for the drink. See you."

Sarah had watched all the CCTV that had captured Lenny's last journey from the B & Q car park to Wandsworth train station. She'd seen him park his new seven series BMW and strut across the tarmac. There weren't many vehicles in the car park, save for a Berlingo van and an open top Volvo V70, with a rotund little man struggling with brass pipes, trying desperately to shove them in the backseat to no effect. Lenny had flashed a look of contempt at the guy as he swaggered past him.

Sarah lost Lenny for a few minutes while he walked to the station. On entering the station, the CCTV caught up with him. Sauntering past, he tossed his head in the camera's direction, and smirked, his sexy trademark grin, openly goading the observer on the other end to "check out the goods." One thing Lenny had had in abundance was brash, brazen, "screw you" confidence.

Scanning the other passengers, Sarah's inspection travelled the length of the platform, flicking at speed to take in other camera angles. She scrutinised every inch of the screen for any sign of the unusual, weird or out of place. But nothing showed up.

Now, Sarah knew what she was looking for had been there all along.

Back at the office, in the media room, Sarah sifted through the tapes and located the one that played on a loop in her mind. There it was. An elderly lady arrived and sat down on the seat towards the middle of the platform. She was directly behind Lenny. Sitting down, she held her trolley tight, and appeared to stare at Lenny.

Sarah selected the area of tape, paused it, and zoomed in on the old woman. Under magnification, her features could be

seen in detail; far from being frail, the old woman looked strong and sturdy, and unusually tall. Her overall posture seemed familiar. *Back straight, collected composure.*

Watching her fiddle with the trolley, Sarah had a sense of darkness, just like the absinth omen that hit her when she'd stopped the bomber outside Canada Water. More than a premonition, much deeper than that, Sarah could perceive the whole story.

The lady had morphed into someone else, but so good was the disguise, Sarah needed more—she couldn't do anything without "hard evidence."

Snapping and printing the screenshot, Sarah slipped it into the case file and hurried to the evidence room. All Lenny's clothes and personal effects had been bagged up, and stored.

"Small like a microdot..."

She remembered what Richard had told her. Sarah searched through everything, scoured every inch of fabric, plastic and paper like a single mother checking her lottery numbers. After two hours of fastidious searching, Sarah came up blank.

"Sod this...," she muttered under her breath, despondency once again taking root. She felt she was so close. Opening the case file, Sarah skimmed the list of effects:

> Mobile phone
> BMW keys
> House keys
> Wad of £50 notes (bank wrapper in situ)
> 2 samples of *Angel Heart* in transparent pocket
> 50 pence in loose change

The £50's were not in the bag. *Where the hell where they?* Sarah looked at the information in the case file and found that DI Sanderson from Serious Organised Crime had taken them. Locating the phone number, Sarah called the DI.

"DI Sanderson..."

"Hello, this is DCI Steiner, Fulham and Chelsea CID, I understand you have a piece of evidence from the Lenny Barlow case."

"The money."

"Well, yes, could I have it back."

"It's evidence as part of a larger investigation into Russian organised crime in London."

"I need it back. I need to check it."

"Okay, I'll send it in the overnighter. But after you're finished with it, can you return it."

Sarah finished with the call, left the office and decided to catch up on some of her DVD box sets. A little touch of coach potato—a little escapism—might actually help her think through her next steps more clearly. If she ever secured the evidence, she would still have to negotiate through the sensitive challenges that such a conviction would bring.

Next morning, Sarah arrived early at police headquarters. There in the centre of her desk, a gem amongst fake stones, sat the overnighter bag. Sarah ripped it open, and huddled inside was the money wad.

Sarah reached for the magnifying glass. A slight smudge on the bank wrapper revealed its RF tag capability. Sarah smiled. Just as Richard had said, a microdot, barely

noticeable to the human eye. This confirmed her theory. It was the evidence she needed.

She photographed the microdot, and had it analysed for its function. The analysis came back, a receiving signal only micro-tag for RFID target purposes only.

Snatching the printout of the analysis, Sarah was ready for closure. Thirty minutes later, she drove up the same winding driveway to the elegant Georgian mansion she'd visited just over a year ago.

She was shown to the Morning Room, and was advised that the owner of the house would not be long. As Sarah waited, she thought about the whole unfortunate business. Sure, she understood. Could even sympathise. That strange look he'd given her should have alerted her, that he'd seek his own vengeance. Why had she been so blind?

Briskly, the door opened and Sir Patrick marched in. His face was gaunt and tired, but still his posture was hard and upright. That stiff upper lip, thought Sarah.

"Please sit down." Sir Patrick touched Sarah's elbow lightly, and then swept his hand towards the sofa.

Sarah sat with a gawky, graceless drop on to the plush cushion. Sir Patrick took the armchair opposite her.

"Sir Patrick, I have come here on delicate business."

"I knew you'd find out." Sir Patrick's words were unexpected, devastatingly honest. His eyes were remote, deadened by the terrors of inhumanity and had, by such excess, become desensitised to the pain.

"You knew?" said Sarah warily. Dealing with Sir Patrick was not like other criminals. He didn't proactively go out and cause crime. Instead, he reacted to it. He had committed grievous bodily harm under extreme duress—and

killed for retribution. But did that make him less guilty, any less accountable for his sins?

"You're a very clever girl. I knew you'd discover the truth. I've been waiting for you."

"Waiting for me?"

"Yes."

"You realize I have to arrest you."

"I know."

"I'm sorry for your loss, for your daughter."

Sir Patrick did not speak. That same look Sarah remembered from the first time she'd met him clouded his face, as though he was caught in time.

"And I'm sorry too..."

"For Lenny Barlow's death?"

"No! For this..."

Suddenly, Sarah felt a wave of nausea engulf her, her chest tightened, she couldn't breathe; as her eyelids drooped she welcomed the onrushing abyss of emptiness.

+

She hadn't a clue on how long she'd been unconscious. On waking, Sarah discovered herself strapped in the driver's seat of her car. Inexplicably, her vehicle was in Richmond Park, facing in the direction of Sheen Gate. Disoriented, Sarah reached for her phone. Her CO came on the line.

"Sir, it's de Laine, he's the killer, he's a tech genius. He used infrasound to kill Lenny Barlow. Get round his place and arrest him."

The CO's words snapped with authority, but Sarah

detected genuine concern for her amongst the sharpness.

"He's gone, Steiner. When you didn't come back I sent the boys round, but de Laine's vanished. So where the hell are you?"

"Gone!" Sarah's voice echoed trembling anger.

"Yes, Steiner, vanished into the proverbial puff. There's an APB out on him. Get back here and explain just what the bloody hell went down!"

"Sir, I can explain. Somehow de Laine hit me with infrasound. I passed out."

Sarah realised as she spoke, de Laine must have targeted her in some way. She recalled the gentlemanly gesture to her arm. She turned her elbow around and there it was. A small, shiny microdot.

"Sir I'll be back soon. My report will detail everything."

Sarah pressed off the phone. Frustration crawled through her. Why hadn't she been more aware? Her quarry had been an exceptional mastermind. And she'd acted as if he was just another criminal. Going into his house without back up. Wanting to take the glory for working it all out by herself. De Laine had played her completely. Deceived her and used her own conceit against her.

Sarah sat back in the car and stared out with despondence. A herd of deer bounded across the park, a sense of freedom outlining their movement; the long stretch of their hind legs as they leaped over the logs and fallen trees; their black eyes shining bright with nature's truth. The stag, magnificent and calm strode over. His posture brought to mind Sir Patrick de Laine. Arrogant and removed, as if distanced from his own kind inherent by power.

The stag turned and glanced at Sarah, his expression one of resolute defiance in the knowledge that he was freer than she would ever be. Tossing back his head, he flew over tree trunks and then disappeared into the woods—at one with himself and the freedom nature afforded him.

Sarah watched him go, and smiled as the irony slapped her.

Just another indifferent male slipping away from her clutches that day.

© *MICHELLE MEDHAT 2016. ALL RIGHTS RESERVED.*

+++

6

THE SCREAM OF SILENCE

Pamela Crane

PART 1

Monday

I came into this life kicking and screaming, and I never stopped since. But a blinking moment is sometimes the only chance we get to turn life around. One opportunity, one shot at redemption. Unfortunately, I had missed my chance...

Her face was contorted in a soundless scream, her skin a sickly marlin blue-gray. My heart caught momentarily, but not in the same fear-struck manner that laboring mothers feel at the sound of nothingness immediately after birth. For me the silence was the gift of relief. Then a breath later her piercing wail shattered that hope.

The wriggling limbs. The squirming body. A sharp cry.

I remember the day well, twenty-three years ago, even though remembrance of last night's dinner was vague: 2:03 a.m., a precise ticking of the clock's hand that announced an

event that would never touch me, yet always haunt me, like prickling fingers running across my naked skin. Fingers that would never let go.

She was a tiny, bald, pinkish creature—all 6 pounds 4 ounces of her. Eyes an iconic Indiglo blue, like her mama's.

Baby Girl Childs.

That was her name, at least according to the flap of paper taped to the transparent plastic bin that the nurses called a bassinet.

The daughter of unwedded, unwanted teenager Destiny Childs. And yes, that's my real name. The famous R&B girl group of the 1990s was not yet a twinkle in the recording studio's eye when my parents named me at the advice of a fortune cookie: "Your destiny will be what you make it." I could imagine it now...

My mother, her overhanging belly quivering as tiny feet slithered beneath her taut skin, in a grimy Chinese takeout booth, cuddling in the crook of my dirt-poor father's armpit. His nails grimy with construction work labor as they discuss baby names over Kung Pao chicken. Then suddenly the answer wrapped in a stale but edible pocket: *Destiny.*

The irony of my name exposed itself unashamedly as life left me far behind. My destiny was little more than a remnant of a lost hope, a sliver of life that I'd never partake in. I'd only watch it from afar, like a foggy dream after being jarred awake. That baby was the only good thing I'd ever do, although I didn't know it back then.

I was glad Baby Girl Childs lost the corrupt part of me that day when her forever family swooped in to rescue her from my ill-equipped clutches, changing her name and

identity. At the time, I was only fifteen and reckless—a "waste of space," a "cold-hearted bitch," a "user and abuser" everyone who knew me or dated me or lived with me said about me. All true. I'm no saint. Wasn't back then, still not now. But part of me hoped I could change that ... just not the biggest part of me. The biggest part of me cared only about me.

Weak, that's what I am.

I never looked back with regret on that day when I pushed Baby Girl away as the nurse held her out to me for one last-chance embrace. "You wanna hold her, honey?"

"No, take her away," I insisted, wiping the sweat of labor from my forehead. Tears streamed down my flushed cheeks, but not for the loss of my child. I cried for myself that day.

Baby Girl Childs was a lifetime-ago memory that I stuffed into the hole in my heart and sealed shut... until I heard her name for the first time in two decades.

Clarissa Beatty.

I knew her name, but she never knew mine. I remembered Eliot and April Beatty from the adoption paperwork, while I remained the shrouded incubation tool tucked behind the red tape. It had been a closed adoption, after all. But I had stalked the Beatty family once upon a time just to check in. Filthy rich. That's what stuck out to me back then.

Now all that stuck with me was the name on the television screen.

I can't remember the last time I watched the news, but Fate was pushing her way in to deliver a message.

The acrid fumes consisting of brake fluid and exhaust

wafted from the Sears Auto Center garage into the cement-block waiting room while the mechanic attempted to revive my POS 2004 Chevy Cavalier on the other side of the floor-to-ceiling window smudged with a collage of greasy handprints. It was a miracle the vehicle even made it to the shop while the billowing cloud of black poured out under the crack of my hood, but $600-I-didn't-have later, I was sitting on a vinyl and metal chair watching my daughter's name flash across the top of the television screen beside a picture of a wide-mouthed smiling brunette:

Clarissa Beatty, 23-year-old murder victim

The chair belched against the concrete floor, plastic suckling my bare legs as I shifted forward in my seat, forcing the revelation upon myself as the news anchor stunned me further:

"Twenty-three-year-old Clarissa Beatty, daughter of Eliot and April Beatty, owners of the locally-owned Beatty's Pest Control franchise, was found dead in her Briar Creek apartment yesterday evening.

"Around ten thirty p.m., authorities responded to a call from Beatty's roommate, Whitney Cardano, when she came home to find Clarissa lying on the floor unresponsive. There was no evidence of a break-in. According to officials, Clarissa was pronounced dead upon their arrival.

"The investigation is ongoing. No information has been released about the circumstances surrounding her death at this time, but police say the incident is being investigated as a homicide."

As the news lady detached herself from an innocent girl's death to shift focus to the devastating plight of Durham, North Carolina's lack of funds for road

improvements, I sifted through my rolodex of feelings: an unfamiliar grieving over something I never had.

It wasn't that I hadn't known grief. I'd had my fair share and then some. A mother dead from a cocaine overdose just as I ventured into adolescence, setting me permanently on the path to failure. A father who turned me into an orphan when he up and left me months later, a shattered and twisted Riddler of a child with nothing but pranks to pull. Theft, prostitution, drugs, depression—my own butterfly cycle.

Life had left me wilted and worn, but my daughter's death became my resurrection.

PART 2
Still Monday

Nerves shuttled from head to toe, churning the stale vending-machine Oreo cookies in my stomach. On the other side of the braggy lion's-mouth door knocker that I thudded against the Brazilian cherry wood, I could only imagine what Eliot and April Beatty were doing. Probably skinny-dipping in their Olympic-sized pool of hundred-dollar bills. Whatever it was, I was sure it was glamorous.

Too many seconds had passed, so I turned to leave. But a *swoosh* of linen-scented air ruffled the hair hanging lifeless down my back—raven black, like my soul.

"Can I help you?" a pitchy voice asked, though without feeling.

I pivoted to face the mournful sound, greeted by a

woman whose gray-streaked ponytail betrayed her supple skin.

"I'm here about Clarissa Beatty. I heard she passed away." Cut to the chase—that was the kind of woman I was.

"And you are—?" she replied, waiting for my answer. One over-tweezed eyebrow shot up in a skeptical checkmark.

"My name is Destiny Childs. I'm her biological mother."

+

Two hours later I had regurgitated my sad story of beginnings and endings—my childhood, unplanned pregnancy, Clarissa's birth, followed by a CliffsNotes version of life after life as I lost a mother and father, skirted through foster families, and eventually fell face-first into a life of chaos. Then I concluded with a semi-morsel of truth: I was now sober.

I omitted that I was only twenty hours in and feeling an overwhelming urge.

I had only needed to excuse myself once to rush to the bathroom in search of something to calm my nerves, since the cucumber finger sandwiches and chamomile tea weren't doing the job. Sure enough, in the vanity I found an orange prescription bottle of Xanax—every trophy wife's secret little helper—with half a dozen 2-mg white oblong pills that would smooth the edges of my sanity. I studied the label. Having been prescribed sixty pills just over a week ago, perhaps I wasn't the one with a problem.

I popped one in my mouth and one in my pocket, in case the visit got much longer. I returned to the great room—and truly it was great, with a cathedral ceiling adorned with polished oak beams and a friggin' stained-glass

skylight—to find palm-sized chocolate mousse tortes garnished with steroid-laden strawberries that I planned to overeat.

"My reason for coming," I finally got around to, "is that I never got to know Clarissa, and part of me regrets it. I guess ... I just want to grieve her. I know I don't deserve this, but ... I dunno how to explain it. Does that make sense?"

Her rosy face bobbed up and down—ponytail causally swinging—as she swiped at tears, then lurched forward to claw me into an overstepping bear hug. "Say no more, sweetie. Of course Clarissa would be honored you are here, that you're thinking of her ... if she knew you were her biological mother, that is."

I pulled back, partly because of the admission and partly because the touchy-feely was making my claustrophobia act up. "She didn't know she was adopted?" I asked.

"Well," April sighed, "we had wanted to find the right time to tell her, but that time never came. It just seemed pointless to crash her world with news like that. It had nothing to do with being ashamed of her past or of you, but we simply never got around to it. I'm sorry to have to tell you that." Pausing, she lifted her pert chin, her eyes saucily scanning me for buried secrets. "But I'm curious—how do you know for sure you're her biological mother? I mean, your story is convincing, but without a DNA test, you can't know 100 percent."

Matching her sass for sass, I stared right back, unflinching. "I'd be happy to take a DNA test to prove it."

My challenge defused the conflict, for April's tension abated as she warmed. "I'm sorry to be so blunt. It's just that with Clarissa's murder and all, I don't know who to trust

anymore. But I would like to take you up on that offer. I hope you're not offended."

"No, it's okay. I understand. I'll do whatever I can to help make things easier on you."

A wobbly smile barely creased April's overfull, unmoving lips, a caricature-esque image incarnate. "You're a doll," she said, her mouth like that of a collagen-addicted ventriloquist's. "I really don't know how you can help ... other than finding who did this to my baby girl. The police don't have any leads other than her boyfriend—*ex*-boyfriend. Seemed like a nice boy to me, from a good family. I don't know why she broke up with him, but one never knows what goes on in a relationship. God knows Clarissa would never tell me things."

So Clarissa instigated the breakup. Was it enough to be a motive for murder?

I checked the thought, pushing it back where it belonged—into the netherworld. I wasn't here to solve a murder. I was here for a much grander scheme.

And then an epiphany alighted upon me—a lightbulb moment, an opportunity-in-waiting. "Well, I'm here for anything you need. Do you need help with planning the funeral? Or what about setting up donations for a cause she was passionate about?" My breath caught in the conversational wake.

April's hazelnut eyes scrutinized me warily, as if assessing the phantom behind a comedy and tragedy mask. I waited for Melpomene to strike, as tragedy always had something against me. But today the Greek muse was MIA.

"What a lovely idea, Destiny. I think she was into saving the polar ice caps. In fact, what if you set up a charity

and handle the accounting for that?"

I had absolutely no idea how one even saved a polar ice cap, but it didn't matter.

"Absolutely. I'm honored. I'll open up a donations account and get you the information. Maybe I can even name the charity after her: The Clarissa Beatty Ice Cap Organization." A laughable tribute, but April was already tearfully on board.

She rose from the sterile-white stiff sofa that clearly cost more than my childhood ghetto townhouse—hell, even my current residence—and briskly strutted to a custom-crafted mahogany rolltop desk. Four-inch Miu Miu peep-toes *click-clicked* across the Italian calacatta marble floors, announcing classiness with every step. Through my Dollar Store turquoise flip-flops (a shade of blue akin to my eyes) I could feel an unnatural warmth rise from the polished limestone. I imagined a two-year-old version of Clarissa sock-skating across the smooth floors, slipping along as gravity—coupled with an indecisive sense of balance—tossed her to and fro.

A bold, bona fide Wassily Kandinsky adorned a two-story wall to one side the room, the abstract shapes and primary colors screaming for attention amid the vast white space. Hideously amateur, I always thought. The handicraft of child's play with a paintbrush, if I hadn't known better—and yes, I'm more cultured than I'm given credit at first glance, a fact belied by my thrift store tank top and ripped jeans.

Clickety-clacking back to me, April held a blue fabric pouch and gold pen, her scribbles scraping against the echoing silence. A tear of paper later, she held out a check.

"How about I make the first donation?"

My flesh ached over the number of zeroes: $10,000.

And thus began the story that would sweep me from Tragedy's grip into the abundant hands of Destiny.

PART 3
Tuesday

Whitney Cardano, Clarissa's lifelong best friend and roommate, talked a mile a minute, only occasionally coming up for air. It was astounding how much the girl could talk without saying anything. But I smiled and nodded—all part of my due diligence.

While a murder investigation wasn't part of my purpose, something about Clarissa's death poked at me, egging me on to figure it out. My earlier stop at the Raleigh Police Department precinct in charge of her investigation was enough to get the bare-bones details that the cops ruled it a murder by alprazolam poisoning. Slipped into her drink, perhaps?

Apparently it wasn't that uncommon, the detective told me. After explaining I was with the family, I insisted on a glimpse of the autopsy report, which contained more information than I knew how to interpret, but the most important findings confirmed my suspicions:

Autopsy: RPD830522-34A
Decedent: Clarissa Beatty
Age: 23

Race: White

Sex: Female

Identified by: fingerprints, dental comparison, family identification

External Examination: Well-developed white female with multiple subdural hematomas, one on right wrist and one on upper arm, demonstrative of a physical altercation.

Toxicology: Blood and vitreous fluid positive for alcohols; blood positive for acidic, basic and neutral drugs (alprazolam)

Cause of Death: Poisoning

Manner of Death: Homicide

The cops had questioned the roommate, who led them to the boyfriend, but with his confirmed alibi, the suspect list was at a standstill. But I wasn't.

That afternoon I decided to visit Whitney at their apartment to see what I could dredge up from her caffeine-befuddled brain. Two empty Starbucks cups sat on the glass-and-chrome coffee table between us, and one shakily in her hand.

Her rear perched on the edge of a vibrant hot-pink sofa that would make Barbie proud as she talked animatedly with her hands, every bit the Italian from the over-gesturing to the teased black hair framing an olive face that had seen one too many tanning booths. Her apartment was anything but typical apartment fare. With easily 1,000 square feet of open gourmet kitchen, a formal tiered-ceiling dining room, and uppity living room space, I could only imagine how much more hid behind the scattered closed doors.

"Clarissa and I, we were besties since kids. Inseparable," Whitney chattered, her line of sight exiting

stage left as if reliving bygone days. A moment later, she returned to Earth fiercely. "I can't believe someone would want to hurt her."

"Any idea who?"

"No, not really. I'm assuming it was some psycho bum or something."

Wow, this girl never ceased to amaze me with her absurdity.

"You think a homeless man followed her home and killed her?"

"Sure, it happens all the time on the news."

Rampant homeless murderers, much like Bigfoot or leprechauns. Her conviction about this version of the truth was unwavering, so I decided to let the idiocy slide. But I was still curious about the men in Clarissa's life.

"What about her boyfriend?"

"You mean her *ex*, Trace Eriksson? God, he was a hottie but a real douchebag. Treated her like he owned her. But killing her—why? He was rich and handsome, could get any girl he wanted... even with that temper of his."

Who names their kid Trace? A frazzled pill-popping soccer mom with her sidekick nanny burst into my head, next to her frat-boy, baseball-playing son with his clean-shaven chiseled jaw and Abercrombie polo.

"What kind of temper?" I asked.

"Just slamming doors and stuff. Hard to ignore, y'know? But they always made up—I could hear it from my bedroom. Ugh. But at least he made her happy ... in his own twisted way. But hey, a guy who looked like that could make any girl happy, if you know what I mean. The boy worked out." Whitney followed this with a mischievous Groucho

Marx eyebrow pop.

I chuckled politely, hoping to stave off further innuendo. "I'm just curious, but what would Clarissa do to make him mad?" My memory ventured back to my parents' fights—how my mom's rampant mood swings would send my dad into a vengeful bottle, not to return to lucidity until the next day. Fights about nothing—the imminent relationship killer.

"Not really sure," she replied with a shrug. "Mostly they blew up when she was having a bad day, I guess. It's like he expected her to be happy all the time. But no one is happy all the time."

It sounded like my memoir. I considered my own struggle with depression, a cycle of frustrated hopelessness revolting against me, waging war on my psyche. Day after day I would be lost in no-man's land, yearning to get out, but too mentally drained to surface to the happy-go-luckys around me. It tossed every relationship I ever had overboard. "Do you think maybe Clarissa was depressed?"

"How would I know?" Whitney gave a halfhearted frown and glanced at her cell phone. "Anywho, sorry I can't help you more, but I got yoga in an hour. Gotta get prettied up." She winked, coupling it with an exaggerated playful smile. "Cute instructor I wanna impress."

What kind of live-in *bestie* didn't know—or care—if her friend was depressed? Perhaps I didn't regret my unpopular status if this was what true friendship consisted of—nothing more than sharing Jimmy Choos and sipping chocolate martinis at hotel bars.

Whitney squeezed me in a brusque hug, my cue to make myself scarce. But I needed something first.

"Do you mind if I use your powder room?" I figured a little snooping wouldn't hurt, though I didn't expect to find anything worthwhile.

"Sure—it's next to the office. I'm going to get a shower, but lock the door as you leave. I don't want to end up next on some hobo's kill list." She pointed a bejeweled fingernail and we parted ways, me treading one way and Whitney sashaying to her private quarters.

As I passed the office, I stepped back in a double take. Several framed pictures of Clarissa sat crookedly on a modern computer desk, a light dusting of grime hovering above the black glass. Peeking over my shoulder into the empty living room, I wandered in. Her father's cartoony smile and mother's pristine teeth greeted me from behind pane after pane. A collage of memories, all vanished in a last breath. Clarissa riding a camel. Clarissa at a bachelorette party. Clarissa bikini-clad with a group of friends at a tropical paradise.

Then an overturned frame, facedown in shame. I flipped it up, my assumptions about Trace spot-on. His hair combed tidily to one side, overpriced collared shirt, handsomely arrogant smile. Almost too good-looking. Possessively clutching an adoring Clarissa, her eyes gazing up at him while he modeled for the camera. The perfect murderer—the classy Brazilian killer Tiago Henrique Gomes da Rocha, or America's charismatic Ted Bundy. Charm oozed from him, the kind of elegance that would reel an unsuspecting girl in for the kill, dare she step out of line.

What line had Clarissa crossed?

As I set it down, I noticed a crack spidering out from the corner of the glass, like tiny legs crawling in search of

prey. Slammed down in rage after a fight? I'd never know.

I skimmed through the remaining pictures, until I came upon one that felt truer, more honest. Just Clarissa, somber and serene. Black and white, gazing sorrowfully at something behind the lens, somewhere beyond space and time. It captured her perpetual beauty... and ultimate sadness. I would know, for I recognized myself in that picture.

It was the image of depression.

And no one knew but me. I heard my own silent scream.

+

REM's "Everybody Hurts" played through my car's CD player as I read Clarissa's flowery prose on the front of *Clarissa's Pity-Party Playlist.* Adorned with morbidly cutesy broken-heart drawings and skull stickers on the homemade case, I had swiped the CD from her room while rummaging through her belongings, looking for something personal that was small enough to fit into my purse. Just something to know her by. A mixed tape—or CD, in this case—seemed as personal an item as any, so I shoved it in my peeling faux leather Goodwill-bought handbag before rushing out the door, lest I get caught.

The opening song surprised me. Clarissa Beatty, rich and popular party girl, seemed more the bubble-gum music variety. Lady Gaga or John Mayer, even. Rock, I hadn't expected. But as I hummed along to the lyrics—for the words had long escaped me—I remembered REM from my own adolescence. An oldie but goodie. Many nights I spent crying into my tear-stained pillow over my latest breakup as

Michael Stipe sang the woes of my heart.

Skipping ahead, the next song was Soundgarden's "Like Suicide." The rock melody described the gilded cage trapping the girl—was this Clarissa? My fingertip tapped the next one in, "Suicidal Dream" by Silverchair. Then Papa Roach's "Last Resort." By this point the theme was catching up to me, and my heart squeezed wildly, as if keeping pace with a hummingbird's wings. Song after song of death and despair, cutting and chaos.

Had Clarissa suffocated under the loss of herself?

Was her death a murder... or suicide?

PART 4
Wednesday

I'm a bad, bad girl.

I do terrible things.

Like framing an innocent man for murder.

Well, let's not get carried away. Trace Eriksson was no victim. An abuser, that's what he was. And like a mama bear—albeit an absentee one—protecting her cub, it was my responsibility to avenge my daughter's death because of what he did to her.

Sure, I knew he hadn't put the pills in her drink. But the cops didn't know April Beatty had just filled a prescription for the same drug that killed Clarissa—something as accessible as Xanax. And they didn't know that Clarissa suffered from undiagnosed and untreated depression. Sure enough, they caught the bruising and battering on the autopsy report, my perfect segue. I may not

have graduated high school, but I knew what a hematoma was. My fascination with *CSI: Miami* paid off.

Now it was Trace's turn to pay.

The plan was foolproof, and I was already knee-deep. Seducing him was simple enough. After looking up his address online, I dolled myself up in a classic black microdress, silver hoop earrings, and enough makeup to pass me for a twenty-eight-year-old. Okay, a twenty-eight-year-old chain smoker. As long as I appeared MILFy enough to grab Trace's gaze, I still had enough hotness to win him over—if it was a slow night for the player. Weren't all Tuesday nights slow at the bar?

I tailed two car lengths behind him from his ritzy Skyhouse Raleigh apartment all the way into downtown Durham, where he left me a little surprised. The bar of choice was a step above a dive, a townsy bistro called Alivia's. Passable fare and a low-key hipster vibe, but nothing as fancy as Trace was dressed for in his black slacks and button-down dress shirt. I admired his ingenuity—a big fish in a small pond. He was out for easy prey.

I'd make sure he hit pay dirt.

The place was loosely packed with a mixture of people, some college-aged drinking newbies and some lifers. A pathway separating two sitting areas led to the open front door. Strings of outdoor lights hung over metal chairs and tables on one side, and fire pits held captive small flames surrounded by laughing patrons on the other. I waltzed through the door, winding my way up to the counter, and wedged myself between Trace and a bleach-blond grandma whose pleated bosom deflatedly poured out of her cinched, sequined top.

"Hey, cutie," I said, resting my hand on Trace's arm. His sleeve was rolled halfway up his forearm, revealing taut muscles and a dusting of hair. "I'm Patty. You are?"

"Trace. Nice to meet you, Patty. Can I buy you a drink?"

I giggled, my hands flirtily gripping him. "I'd love one. Surprise me."

He ordered me a Cosmo and himself a Scotch. Typical choice.

"You come here often?" I probed. I needed to know where he had been Sunday night if I was going to execute, but I needed to apply the pressure evenly.

"Yeah, but I've never seen you here."

"I was just here on Sunday. You missed a good time," I teased, my palm squeezing his thigh.

"Sorry, that night I was at the Person Street Bar. Ever been there?"

And it was that easy—Trace had no idea how easy a mark he was.

Three hours and four mixed drinks later, I tossed my black lace thong under Trace's bed, far enough back that he'd never notice but that a police investigation would turn it up easily. Tiptoeing out the door with my stilettos in hand—damn, those shoes were torture!—I skipped through the wee-morning coolness, adding an air-kick-of-my-heels, exploding with the first semblance of pure joy I'd had in a long time.

Glancing up and down the silent street, with only a streetlight illuminating my car, no one witnessed my "walk of shame"—or whatever the antithesis of that was, in my case—as they slept in pillow-hugging huddles beneath their

down comforters. Sleep was something I didn't anticipate tonight.

Perhaps it was my foray into motherhood that gave me such pleasure, or the simple act of eating the rich, but whatever it was, I was addicted. And the game had only just begun.

PART 5
Thursday

"Yes, detective, I can give a statement about the night of Clarissa Beatty's murder."

In jumbling detail, I had exhaustively explained to Detective Moody that yes, I had come into the police station two days ago. And yes, I hadn't been honest about who I was. No, not family but a woman who knew Trace Eriksson. Yes, I had tried to get information about the Beatty murder, because yes, I had a tip about who might have killed her. And yes, I had met Trace at the Person Street Bar that night and we left together for his apartment. No, he wasn't there all night but left early that evening.

"So," Detective Moody said, heaving a hefty breath, "you're telling me that the night of Clarissa's death you were with Trace in his apartment. Then he left around 7:00 p.m. to, and I quote, 'take care of some business regarding his ex.' That's what he said?"

"That's correct," I affirmed. "I assumed it was nothing, until I saw her name on the news. We had talked about exes during our conversation that night and he mentioned her name."

Lie after lie escalated the story, delving into depths I didn't know were there. All believably validated and orchestrated by yours truly. Even I was convinced.

"Well, this does line up with his alibi. I'll check into it. If you could write down everything you've just told me, that will help us a lot. Thank you, Miss Childs."

The detective handed me a yellow legal pad and pen, then left me to spend the next thirty minutes uncomfortably sliding back and forth on my metal folding chair as I wrote the most exquisitely sinister lie of my life.

Clarissa's bruises.

A witness testimony debunking Trace's alibi.

And the grand finale: proof—my underwear under his bed.

I had the girlfriend-beating bastard cornered.

PART 6
Friday

April Beatty's tears watered her brown orbs as we sat cattycorner on matching cushioned wicker chairs under her back veranda. A light breeze from an overhead fan stuck wisps of ebony hair in my lip-gloss, which I pried gently away and tucked behind my ear.

"I'm so sorry about any pain this caused you. I really thought I was Clarissa's biological mother, but it turns out I'm not." I had just arrived at the Beatty estate—for an estate was the only proper word to describe the quasi-mansion on ten acres—with the difficult news.

"Perhaps it's better this way," April said. She folded

one leg over the other, her navy pumps hidden beneath the hem of her beige linen pants. "I mean, you didn't lose a daughter after all. I'm suffering this loss alone... well, Eliot and I. But I'm glad for you." She grinned wearily, a despondent burden that her lip injections couldn't carry.

"Well, it still hurts my heart to think of any mother going through this. But from what I read, they arrested Trace Eriksson. Sounds like her killer may be caught after all. I hope that gives you peace."

The front-page article in *The News and Observer* was sprawled open on an end table adjacent to us. A bowl of fruit salad and honey-sweetened yogurt lay untouched next to two china cups of tea on saucers.

The Beatty Murder Suspect Now in Custody

According to the Raleigh Police Department, investigators have arrested Trace Eriksson, ex-boyfriend of 23-year-old murder victim, Clarissa Beatty, of Raleigh.

Eriksson, 28, is accused of poisoning Beatty in her Briar Creek apartment at around 7:00 p.m. on Sunday. Due to witness testimony and undisclosed evidence, Eriksson was picked up by police and is scheduled to have his first court hearing on Thursday.

After being questioned, Eriksson was transported to the Wake County Detention Center and charged with murder. He remains in custody with bond still pending.

With trembling fingertips, April traced the headline that lurked along the edge of her vision. "Yes, yes it does give me peace that Trace is getting what's coming to him. I

hope he rots in jail." She exhaled the pent-up anger. "But at least we can put her to rest now. That's all that matters."

"You'll be in my thoughts, April. Take care of yourself."

As I rose, she sat sadly stoic, a breakdown away from losing herself. So I did something I didn't know I was capable of doing. Reaching over, I placed my arm around her, drawing her to me. Kissing her forehead, my embrace vented the sorrow as she wept into my shoulder. A simple gesture soothed her broken spirit as I held her, letting the pain seep into the tear-stained fabric.

Despite the lies to April, to the police, despite my compulsion to run away and forget everything all over again, right now I would be a friend.

+

The nondescript cream envelope sat on my kitchen table, hiding under two days' worth of junk mail. LabCorp's address hung in the top left corner, partially missing from when I had torn open the letter two days ago.

I shuffled the heap aside, retrieving it for a final look before tossing it in the garbage. I didn't want the reminder. A loneliness etched across my heart as I looked down at the paper. It was official: I was no longer a mother.

With 99.98% certainty, I was Clarissa Beatty's biological mother.

I had a dead daughter.

My deceit had become a nasty four-letter word, everything from the past week a sham. But not without purpose.

I hadn't planned it this way. I had wanted to tell the truth ... but only part of it. It was a selfless act, deceiving April about the DNA test results. With the shared bond of motherhood, I could never hide Clarissa's true cause of death from her: suicide. But what mother wants to discover that her own child *killed herself?* Murder was a far better option. I had to let her believe that, for her own sanity. But to do it, I knew I needed to walk away forever, and bear the burden of this truth alone.

Guilt was a relentless son of a bitch. Cut all ties to keep my lies.

It was better for everyone ... right?

With a whispered good-bye, I fisted the paper into a ball and tossed it in the garbage can, along with some other advertisements and the shredded remains of April's $10,000 check.

Yes, I had surrendered the conspirator in me when I lost the daughter I'd forgotten and clung to the better parts of her, the parts that maybe she did get from me after all. No more deceit. Kill the parasite within me. That would become my mantra. Because of her, it was my destiny to be a better Destiny. A death not in vain.

But I knew I couldn't do it alone.

Fate was hard at work.

Despite my every effort to protect Clarissa from my demons of depression, she could not escape her hereditary fate.

I wanted to scream. At the injustice of her life in the ungrateful hands of an abuser. At the tragedy of her suicide. At her unspoken hopeless despair. I just wanted to scream, which I could no longer do in silence.

A fitting blue pamphlet I happened upon had made it onto my table, and it appeared to be the answer to my prayers:

Are you struggling with depression? Have you, or someone you know, contemplated suicide? Has suicide taken the life of someone you love? Join us at the Suicide Support Group to meet others who share your burden, and find relief from the pain.

Weekly group meetings. Contact for more information.

I would go.
And I would find peace... even if it killed me.

+

Destiny's journey is just beginning in this prequel to *The Little Things That Kill Series*. For more details on the next book in the series, visit **www.pamelacrane.com**.

© PAMELA CRANE 2016. ALL RIGHTS RESERVED.
+++

7

MARK OF THE HYENA

Mark Fine

N!xau shifted his tiny shadow with an uneasy shuffle of feet. From the moment he spotted the uneven footprints in the rusted sand, he knew it meant trouble. A pity that the Oryx antelope they were hunting had veered this way. If only it turned west, toward home. Now that the stranger's spoor was known, they couldn't turn back.

With an irritated click of his tongue N!xau instructed his hunting party to hold their position. Cautiously, he advanced on the still form partially coated by clinging African earth. Was the stranger still living? He looked up into the blazing sun as though questioning the wisdom of the creator, /Kaggen. The glare back carved heavy shadows across the deep ridges of N!xau's prematurely aging face. Neither his god nor the wisdom of his years dispelled his disquiet.

The Oryx antelope that had gotten away was a magnificent creature. It stood tall—shoulder-to-shoulder—to

that of a grown man. Its horns above a striking black and white masked face stood straight and long—the length of a man's outstretched arms. That single animal would have filled the bellies of all 24 members of his tight-knit band.

Why my people should need to starve for this? He gestured with futility at the fallen figure.

N!xau looked closer at the lifeless stranger lying at his feet. The once pale face topped with spiked russet hair was now a blotch of scabs, scrappy beard, and lips cracked deep with raw fissures.

The size of the man lying baking in the desert sun was immense.

He had never seen such a giant. He, N!xau, was the tallest of his tribe, standing at five foot four inches. Yet, he expected his forehead would only reach the base of the man's chest.

The San Bushman considered his options. Food was his first concern. The loss of that Oryx was unlucky. He had promised his people fresh meat, instead, some of his tribe would have to make do with an */inidzi* meal of dried grasshoppers and crickets tonight, he thought ruefully.

His other concern was his beliefs—a synthesis of material and spiritual lore. This pale, blotch-stained man had the mark of the hyena, a lesser god—the creature of death.

Troubled, N!xau shifted his feet again.

The cool haven of shade from N!xau's shadow now shielded the stranger's face from the sun. The result—a groan and pained grimace.

The big man was alive.

Werner's seared eyelids flickered open. A cloud of biting flies took flight, their encrusted feeding ground now disturbed. The shade protecting his eyes momentarily lifted, replaced with the harsh glare of the sun. Then, an eclipse of sort again brought relief. It took a moment for Werner to comprehend that a bobbing human head was the unreliable source of shade.

Won't the damn idiot just stand still?

His irritation grew with the jabbering of excited 'clicks' and 'clups' from the mouths of a dozen diminutive people. Irritation turned to alarm. He was surrounded. And they were armed. Each man carried a primitive arsenal; a bow, arrows in a bark quiver, and club or spear.

Werner realized this wasn't an esoteric social science program anymore. This was horribly real. All his puffed up theories and methodologies were a sudden abstraction, and simply, redundant.

Here he was, a modern Gulliver—all six feet four inches tall, with red hair, sun-shy pale skin, the stain of dried sweat around his back and belly—lying on the parched ground surrounded by these African Lilliputians.

No, this journey had become a fucking disaster.

All because of a bet ... a bet he lost. Though Werner hated to admit it.

His colleagues considered him an arrogant prig. Werner embraced their scorn. The trick was to sell them on the notion of his cerebral superiority. Facts were irrelevant. A pity, this, for he was not an ignorant man, having gained tenure on merit. Instead, the associate professor had slipped into an intellectual malaise. He now rested on his laurels, and chose to overwhelm all challengers solely with a blizzard

of verbose obfuscation. Supercilious, as ever, Werner declared the San Bushmen to be 'inept primitives.' He gleefully mocked their verbal tradition and oral history. Certainly, a people who relied on campfire songs and storytelling pantomimes as the means to pass down the wisdom of the ages, to future generations was seriously flawed—in his esteemed opinion.

Werner had ranted on. He claimed little patience for a society that failed to document its history, culture and traditions on parchment, paper, and pen. In fact, as the San had no literary accomplishments, they were to him a trivial people. Smug, Werner deemed the case closed. Then, a colleague disputed his allegation that the San had never documented their legend.

Werner protested. His colleague argued. A challenge was proffered and wager agreed. Oh, how he regretted that moment.

Once confronted with the evidence—the Googled *National Geographic* images presenting a rich vein of extraordinary rock artworks, rendered by ancient San people, proved conclusive—a churlish Werner conceded defeat. With the wager lost, he planned to wriggle out of the bargain by pleading poverty. However, the Dean thwarted his scheme by ensuring that the college would underwrite his research trip costs to sub-Saharan Africa. Compelled to honor his obligation, the professor tried to put on a brave face. Being a renowned stickler for creature comforts, his fellow instructors rejoiced at the prospect of him "roughing it" in grimy Africa. When Werner shipped off there was surprisingly little fanfare, his final memory a feeble "Dr. Livingstone, I presume?" joke.

The San hunting party had come upon the green machine wrecked deep in a *donga*—a ravine. In his native tongue N!xau had no word for the color 'green.'

Later, around the campfire, he would tell the story about the destroyed vehicle that was 'the color of fresh grass.' In a flurry of gestures and verbal clicks, his band would wistfully express their need for rain; it'd been nine months since the barren desert had last borne a single blade of green grass.

With luminous thorn pricks of the starred Milky Way trailing across the pitch black sky, N!xau would continue to elaborate on the day's events. It was a rich tale told in mimicry, song, dance, and a staccato of clicks.

His audience would be entranced. Their wide-eyed faces flickered burnt orange around the communal flame.

He told of the abandoned vehicle and the brief time it took to find the injured man. After all, it was a simple task, with blood drops from a broken nose easy to follow. Also, the pale giant had traveled a long time but had not gone far in distance. The unsteady spiral of footprints etched in the desert sand told a story of confused desperation. As bush craft experts, to the San this was familiar; it was the pattern of prey as it faltered to the hunter's poisoned arrow.

The patience of hunters. It is survival's key. For N!xau it could mean a relentless fifty-hour chase on foot to snare an antelope, the moment it succumbed to his poisoned arrow—before hyena and vulture violated his kill.

But not this day. No chase. No kill. There would be

no food. Instead of the band carrying meat back to the camp, in time for the evening meal, they would return with an uninvited guest, this pale giant.

N!xau's wife, K/ora would not be pleased. As the prime gatherer, she was a tough taskmaster. But understand, she would. Not so !Xi. The child would be crestfallen at what he perceived as a promise broken. But all was not lost, as a lesson would be learned. !Xi would now understand that the sanctity of life, even that of a stranger, was more valuable than possessions.

However, N!xau would forgive his son's disappointment as he remembered the rite of passage well. For it remained a proud memory, the day his father blessed him with his first real bow with sharpened arrows. But, without fresh hide, bone, and sinew from this hunt, N!xau feared his promise to his boy would be delayed—

Unless I can craft a bow from an old weapon of mine to fit the boy...

+

On the transatlantic flight over, Werner read an in-flight magazine article about San as cunning hunters. What he read surprised him. Apparently, despite being inveterate predators, the bushmen did their best to avoid killing the female and the young of their prey. To them, survival of the species was mutually beneficial. *Such evolved primitives*, Werner thought, aware of the irony.

His theories of *developed* versus *primitive*, as preconceived as they were, had taken a knock, and he

resented it. In the same well-thumbed periodical, he saw stunning photographs of San rock art discovered in the crags of South Africa's Drakensberg Mountains.

The professor saw three thousand years of San history richly told in pigmented colors of Hematite browns, bloody reds, ochre yellows, and zinc oxide whites. Adding distinctive richness were rich blacks of charcoal and soot. Rather than primitive, stick figures, he was delighted by the depth and artistry of the drawings—especially the dynamic interpretation of the human form. The umber silhouette figures frolicked. They reminded him of Henri Matisse's early 20th Century masterpiece *Dance (La Danse.1)*. A similar sense of movement and fluid grace was apparent in both the San rock art and Matisse's grand work hanging in Manhattan's Museum of Modern Art.

Though Werner had no proof the Fauvist master had ever seen San Bushman rock paintings, he knew of Matisse's fascination with primitive art, and now understood a connection was plausible.

The painted cave walls depicted great floods, horrific battles, and epic game hunts. Werner learned of these and other things. The dual role of the great eland antelope in San lore; the animal served as the supreme shape-shifting sky god, and the earthly creature that embodied fresh food and warm clothing.

Werner saw this animal reverently rendered as the spiritual god it embodied—the essence of life's rituals, yet, he also saw images of the same animal resolutely hunted as the prime source of nourishment.

Indeed, the San people had vividly documented their legend in a substantive way beyond mere oral tradition.

Moreover, in a manner more vibrant than the written word. There was no disputing it. However, Werner could never admit it to his colleagues. With a sullen grunt, he ripped the pages of San rock art from the airline's publication.

Werner drove the Kelly green Toyota Land Cruiser along 1,800 kilometres of mostly dusty, corrugated roads from KwaZulu-Natal to the Kalahari Desert. The sticky tropical climate of the South African east coast with its boisterous plant life, the huge striped leaf of the *Canna Durban* and pineapple shaped palms gave way to fields of sugarcane and sisal plants. Eventually sumptuous greens gave way to semi-lifeless browns of shifting dunes and savanna scrub of the southerly west coast.

Sure, he hadn't volunteered for this mission, but since he'd been compelled to do so, it was professional pride, and an abiding hope to prove his detractors wrong, that persuaded Werner to conduct some semblance of research.

By default a skeptic, the professorial Werner was not prepared to accept the sublime *'NatGeofication'* of Africa— the magazine's magnificent photography and stirring narrative seemed to romanticize the region, turning a blind eye to the scourge of tribalism, blight, poaching and poverty.

Yet, an adolescent Werner had once enthusiastically embraced yellow-framed copies of the famed magazine. Uncomfortably, he recalled how the bare-breasted Nubian women within its pages had once enthralled him.

As the unwavering horizon maintained its distance, the professor wrestled with boredom. Strange for an academic, supposedly curious about the world he lived in.

But, it was thirst, caused by the arid wilderness, that made him careless.

He drank a local Lion Lager beer, then another. What harm? There was no other traffic except for the odd donkey cart.

Unexpectedly, his vehicle found its way into a *donga*—an eroded gully.

Thirst. His damn thirst got him into trouble. Now it was killing him.

He gestured for water.

Their response angered him; more mouths clucked nonsense back at him, and then, as if disinterested they wandered away!

Werner attempted to summon them back, but no intelligible sound past his parched lips.

A new sound alarmed him. With his cheek wedged against the earth, it was difficult to rotate his head, but fear of the unknown trumped the pain and so his large head swivelled.

Now he could see them. They were digging with long sticks.

Was it to be his shallow grave?

Then there was an enthusiastic clap-clap of hands, as the Bushmen surrounded one of their own in communal solidarity.

With the figure at the center hidden from view, Werner relied on his hearing. There was a furious scraping sound of hard wood on softer vegetation.

Was it to be his burial shroud?

Werner wasn't prepared to die, especially not this way;

anonymous, and at the hand of these trivial people.

In his turquoise nautical-themed Bermuda shirt, Khaki shorts, and suede Chukka boots he lay there, helpless; his severe dehydration prevented any chance of escape.

How he loathed them. *They* were the cause of this misadventure.

His anxiety reached a breaking point when twelve small men, clothed only in animal hide loin cloths decorated with ostrich shell beads, advanced toward him.

Werner attempted to screech for his life, but from his dry throat came only a croak.

The San chuckled. Amusement reached the deep creases surrounding their eyes.

A clenched fist was thrust in his face—with thumbs-down—the gladiatorial symbol of a condemned man (Oh shit!).

Werner flinched. Then a miracle happened.

The sweet taste of water from the "bushman melon"—the bulbous root of the *Tsama* plant—trickled past his lips and down his throat. More precious water, squeezed from root shavings, dripped from N!xau's downturned thumb.

Werner drank greedily, as clan-members filled ostrich eggshell containers with precious water to take with them.

Relieved, Werner looked up at N!xau. His gratitude pivoted to annoyance. He was being ignored. The San had his head tilted west toward the setting sun as if feeling the tug of home.

After a slow and deliberate hydration, the San hunters helped the professor to his unsteady feet. Then they offered him a tall stick for balance, which Werner accepted with a grunt.

Apparently, it was time to go home—wherever the dickens their damn home was.

The demented chuff of a distant hyena stirred the San camp to life. Still blessedly mild in the early morning cool, the sun glimmered between the veins of branches and thatch that framed the simple dwelling. His hosts' hut was one of nine that formed a ring around the hearth at the heart of the camp.

Through the doorway—so low he had to bow fully at the waist to enter, Werner saw N!xau and his son, !Xi team up to light the fire. As the stick whirred between caloused hands with a wha... wha... wha... the young boy blew on the smouldering tinder. Soon father and son's faces lit up from shared satisfaction as the first flames greeted the new day—in time for the morning meal.

As he reached for the calabash of water on the earthern floor beside him, Werner noticed that the diminutive hunter had slept with his bow and quiver of arrows beside him. Alongside it lay a small replica; the child's bow and arrow N!xau had promised his son.

Spoilt brat. That toy bow and arrow set was such a waste of the elder Bushman's time.

Irritable, Werner sipped carefully—his mouth and throat hurt. Still fidgety, he found the magazine article he'd 'borrowed' from the plane crammed in his pocket. The rock art imagery still surprised him.

Putting on his best professorial airs—difficult without reading glasses and with his bum flat on the ground—Werner read the commentary by famed South African author, *Laurens van der Post*.

"His paintings show him clearly to be illuminated with spirit; the lamp may have been antique, but the oil is authentic and timeless, the flame was well and tenderly lit. He, alone of all the races in Africa, was so much of its earth and innermost being that he tried constantly to glorify it by adorning its stones and decorating its rocks with paintings. We other races went through Africa like locusts devouring and stripping the land for what we could get out of it. The Bushman was there solely because he belonged to it."

N!xau snatched the pages from the white man's grasp. He did not understanding this trickery. Was this giant with hair the color of dried blood a shaman? Or, was the praying mantis god, /Kaggen, testing him? He squeezed his eyes shut, his brow a concertina of wrinkles. Then opened them, warily. Nothing had changed.

Somehow their sacred animal, the eland, had freed itself from the rock cave wall and placed itself on the 'leaves' now gripped in his hands.

The little man trembled. His wonderful wife was expecting a baby. Normally joyful news, it was a crisis in these times of severe drought. It must be K/ora's untimely fertility in this barren wilderness that had angered the gods.

The San elder knew what needed to be done...

Avoiding the pale giant's stern glare, N!xau retrieved his bow and quiver of arrows from its secure place beside his sleeping kaross. Quietly, so as not to further annoy the unsettling stranger in his home, N!xau slipped over his lean shoulder a crude leather bag topped up with supplies for the game hunt.

Only the rich fat taken from a freshly killed eland's throat, and prepared as a broth—a potent symbol of beauty and abundance—would soothe the riled gods.

K/ora fussed over Werner. Gently she re-applied a soothing poultice of Kraal Aloe to his sun-seared body. As she labored away, K/ora gave a cheerful commentary in the implosive consonants and clicks of the San—a merry stream of cork-popping noises and "tsk-tsk" exclamations. Though he still didn't understand her jabbering, it no longer irritated him. It seemed, somehow ... mellifluous. Odd, neither did the scent of her bother him anymore. Among the skyscrapers back home, her smell would have nauseated him. Yet, this feral mix of hearth smoke, cooked animal fat, sweat and gathered herbs strangely enticed him—echoes, possibly, of those long ago dog-eared copies of NatGeo magazine.

Werner's painful skin made him aware of hers. It was a deep caramelized-yellow, so sheer and smooth despite her harsh life. Then he studied the serene face beneath hair coiled in tufted patterns. Her barely lobeless ears framed high cheekbones that lifted her eyes into the shape of almonds grown near the Yamuna River in India. The hint of Asia found here, in this remote heart of Africa, further intrigued him.

Doesn't she realize how lovely she is? Of course not. She knows nothing about a mirror... imagine, she's never seen her own reflection. As K/ora administered to his exposed sores, Werner enjoyed her cool touch. Her petite stature, reminded him of long-ago teenage loves—forbidden, vulnerable. Maybe exotic. It aroused him.

Imperiously, Werner reached for her with the sense of entitlement of his kind. He grasped her wrist. It mattered not that she trembled, for the associate professor of social sciences—with the hubris of a tenured, soulless career in academia—well understood that the San woman perceived him to be a god.

Lust blinds jingoism and elitism: Strange thing, that.

Superior he was; numb to the betrayal of the man that saved his life and the shelter he had received. His callous seduction a primitive rebuttal to all that was civilized.

These people had nothing. Yet Werner took for himself the only thing they cherished.

Quietly K/ora submitted. Though a sense of hopelessness pierced her soul, what was she to do? If she did not comply, what horrors would this god visit upon them? Disease. Famine. Death.

Selflessly K/ora sacrificed the sanctity of her home, and fealty to her husband, and her intimate self in the hope of appeasing this bleached giant. She'd never before in her life seen a man so pale—so he had to be a god, sent to bring rain to the parched earth.

Therefore, she complied. Thankfully, the act was not unduly violent.

!Xi saw the anguish on his mother's face through a gap in the fretwork of their thatched hut. Eager to play with the bow and arrow his father had made for him, he'd come by his home to prepare it for rat hunting.

His childlike delight was shattered by the rutting of the pasty-faced stranger, with hair the color of mud.

Knowing wildlife behavior in the bush, he was familiar with nature's coupling. However, the assault on his mother was harsher than animals in the wild.

!Xi understood the violation. It angered him.

+

Dig. Dig. The crude stick tore at his fingers as he pounded at the earth. Blisters burst as they formed on !Xi's young hands, not yet weathered by life's experience. What he was seeking should be at the base of this myrrh tree, but the hole was already two feet deep with nothing to see but coarse sand and plant roots.

This slight deciduous tree was normally a treat for him to visit, as its roots were sweet. At times, it solved a host of maladies: the fruit settled his bellyaches, the bark fended off malaria, and the resin—once burnt, was an insecticide. And, if the male elders were to be believed (he often snooped as they chattered), it even excited their animal desires. Not that he understood the meaning of *that*, but no matter, today he had a special task. Not the tree itself, but larva of the Leaf beetle burrowed beneath.

The boy paused. In an updraft column of parched air, a kettle of inquisitive vultures circled overhead. Protecting his eyes from the sun with a tired hand !Xi inspected the horizon, as if wary of discovery, and then continued with his search.

+

Even in this god-forsaken desert, removed from any modern accoutrements, a rickety bus does sometimes drive by. This is my lucky day, cheered Werner!

If Werner understood correctly his host's ridiculous gesticulations, N!xau needed to track down a wounded antelope so the native's son would be his escort to the road. This tested his patience. He had pretended enough to be that snotty-nosed kid's buddy.

In the hope of bringing to future San a written tradition—and strong anecdotal data to buttress his nascent research, Werner had attempted to teach the boy the rudiments of writing and math. With a stick, he'd scratched countless numerals and letters in the desert sand. Yet, his effort proved futile, as the boy frustratingly erased his work in flurries of indignant clicks. Apparently, the silly child had ironically mistaken his earnest letterings as primitive renderings of superior San rock art.

Werner knew this because !Xi, now familiar with the in-flight magazine pages, tapped at the photographs of rock paintings, giggled, and then shook his head as he pointed to Werner's desert floor scratchings.

Time to get outta here—and back to civilization.

Nothing to pack, Werner did a quick inventory of his body. A snort under his rank armpits confirmed the need for a long, cool shower. Protectively he patted the pockets of his stained khaki shorts; yes, his wallet was still there. Uncharacteristically, he thought to give the San family some money—but quickly discarded the notion; after all, they'd have little use for it.

Lost in thought, considering the bleakness of a world where money held no value, Werner was suddenly startled.

Dead-on behind him stood young !Xi, the finger he'd used to prod Werner's ribs still raised. In his other hand, the boy held the small bow and quiver of arrows his father had created for him.

As though they were about to embark on some grand adventure, the boy excitedly ambushed Werner with a fusillade of vocal clicks and hand signals. He thrust toward Werner his proudest possession, the bowed weapon, as if seeking a demigod's blessing.

"A mere toy, it wouldn't hurt an ant," scoffed the pale professor.

The child seemed to understand the mocking tone. He stared up at the giant and challenged him with a simple offering—a shaft tipped with an arrowhead fashioned from animal bone.

Come. Test the arrow's point. I dare you.

Werner could not resist. Again, he had to have the last word; the lost bet with a know-it-all colleague long forgotten. With a large freckled thumb, a patronizing Werner tapped the tip. Startled, he whipped his hand back.

"Ouch, that's bloody sharp!"

An engorged tick of blood beaded up on Werner's thumb. Shrugging nonchalantly he sucked the evidence away, but not before noticing the smirk on !Xi's face. The boy hadn't laughed but in the nearby wilderness Werner heard a hyena chatter with glee. Inexplicably afraid, the need to catch that bus, now, overwhelmed the social science guru.

Meekly he followed the San child—walking silently on naked feet—toward his lost roadway.

+

N!xau barked out to his son. The boy rushed up, eager to please. Playing with other kids was fun, especially the hooked-knee roundabout game. But today !Xi felt grown-up. He felt ready to join the circle of adults: but to do so he must hunt, and get his first kill.

His father invited him to sit down with a quick pat of the flinty earth. Dutifully !Xi settled on his haunches and listened.

"//Son, fetch your arrows," said N!xau. "I must teach you how to add the poison. No poison and your first eland won't fall—your bow is too weak to kill it with one blow."

"Already did the poison, !Pa." Seeing a frown shade his father's eyes, the boy added, "I wanted to surprise you."

"*How...*"

Uncertain whether it was a question, or surprised exclamation, the young San cautiously explained, "!Pa, I watch you closely when you make poison. I know to dig beneath the myrrh tree. Then find the beetle larva. Then squeeze the grub's guts into a sticky mix of sap and spit."

Unconvinced, N!xau asked, "Did you remember *not* to poison the arrow's tip?" He went on to tell how the San smeared the poison a little higher up the arrow shaft. The San elder glanced at his son's face, it was hard to read—as if maturity had suddenly replaced the openness of youth.

Or, was there something else...?

!Xi's father explained. "You must be careful," he warned. "You don't want to knick yourself by mistake. The smallest prick of poison into your bloodstream will kill you..."

As if grateful for having shared in the secrets of his people, the young San Bushman remained quiet.

Then !Xi's face brightened.

"!Pa, how long does it take an antelope the size of a large man to die?"

"My //son, it takes two settings of the sun to kill such an animal. Why do you ask?"

"!Pa, what animals did you hunt when you were my age?"

"I only hunted rats with my first bow, my child. I know you wish to please me, but hunting a big antelope is dangerous."

"Oh, nothing like that, !Pa. I have already gotten me a *rat*. You need not worry."

Hearing a cackle behind him, !Xi leaped to his feet. In a flurry of handclaps and screeches, the San youngster chased away the creature sniffing around the dying embers of the family fire. The hyena growled resentment, its dark spiteful eyes locked onto !Xi's—challenging the boy—then it slunk away into the gloom of the desert's sunset.

© Mark Fine 2016. All rights reserved.

+++

8

BENEATH

Anita Kovacevic

My fingers felt the silk of my daughter's hair as I twisted the golden waves into an elegant, loose bun for her husband's charity event. Her hair no longer smelled of peach baby shampoo, and the skin on her neck glistened from expensive lotions, sprinkled with rich perfume. She was over thirty now, but her skin still looked lovely; all those sacrifices I'd made as a mother had paid off. Memories overflowed my mind and I sighed.

+

She had always been quite average, never a scholar or a real beauty. We named her Isabella, an exaggerated name in a feeble attempt to disguise the fact that she was not a pretty baby, or wanted, for that matter - a boy would have been so much easier for my husband, Geoffrey, to accept. This way, he just kept away, consoling himself with a sip of rum every

day, poor man; there is never much a man can do with a daughter anyway.

Mind you, Isabella hadn't made my job easy; I had so little to work with, and giving birth to the little damsel had ruined my chances of having another child. She sure did a number on both her parents - turning her father into a depressed man with an alcohol issue, and her mother into a barren, self-sacrificing educator. At least we saved up on education - providing her with one would not have made much of a difference. I taught her the basics; any more than that would have given her all sorts of ideas, things that her poor mind could not have handled.

However, I managed to train her to know her place, keep her mouth shut and act like a demure lady. I had no idea why she was always so moody as a child, constantly asking questions other girls never would. After all, I did get her hair done daily at my salon, and new dresses and manicures, no charge at all. I went with her to church, and took care of all her doctor's appointments, so that one day she could do her wifely duty for her husband and become a mother.

No need to tell you about the hard times she gave me - disciplining her had become such a nuisance that I kept a closet empty at the backroom of the salon, where I could shut her in on busy days. I ran a tight ship so we had plenty of busy days. At first she would cry and scream, but I found the sleeping pills Dr Jensen had once prescribed for Geoffrey's insomnia particularly useful for calming down her tantrums.

"Keep quiet and you'll be safe," I'd always tell her, just before locking her up.

The threat of *"or else"* was never necessary – she knew what would happen.

+

Eventually, my efforts paid off and she did get married. At least she was good enough for that. A fine husband I found her, too. It took quite an effort on my part to find someone out of town, but I finally got lucky when I went to the city for some blood tests. I stumbled into a nice, young doctor from a highly traditional family who completely understood my problems. He even smiled when I showed him a picture of my wretched child. Dr Howard Dean! What a wonderful name! Some sort of an angel had put that man in my path and, eventually, he offered to ease this mother's troubles and take Isabella for his wife.

Dr Dean was considerate enough to promise a yearly donation to my husband and me for all our troubles of raising her, and we were kindly informed there would be no need to visit her much. He would now take care of her sedative addiction; he was a doctor after all. In the case of grandchildren, we would not be expected to play the role of traditional caring grandparents, seeing as Isabella had already taken such a toll on us. Howard even paid for an elegant wedding and I looked grand in my burgundy silk gown with the turquoise necklace my son-in-law had gifted me.

Isabella got through the entire thing without a word. I'd told her that she wouldn't be seeing much of me after she moved to her husband's home, and she must have been torn, the poor soul. I followed her progress in the society

pages, and was the envy of our town when her picture appeared in the papers. For some ridiculous reason, the media thought she was pretty. Still, Howard had taken my advice and never let her do any interviews, which was for the best, I am sure.

+

Just look at her now - my baby girl, all grown-up, a high-society lady, married to an esteemed doctor and mother of four, and I still so young and vibrant, despite all the hardship she'd put me through. What more could I have hoped for? And where has time perished? Such a shame Geoffrey was gone to visit his relatives on the other side of the country - I wanted to show him how much good my education had brought to our daughter.

She was sitting in that chair, a still image, like so many times before when she was a girl. She acted with serenity, her posture was perfect, her breathing shallow but rhythmical, her hands placed in her lap, her legs crossed below her knees... just a picture perfect, high-society woman of substance, the way I'd made her into.

But a mother knows when something is different.

How did I know? She was here, in my hair salon, when she could be have been having her hair done by any of the posh stylists who are always on call for the rich and famous. There's a list of them at her beck-and-call, and each would leap at the chance to add their indelible touch to Mrs. Dean's hairstyle.

And there was something else, too, something that made my skin crawl. From time to time, she'd look up at the

mirror and look directly into my eyes. Directly! She knew better than to do that; she was obviously slipping.

Something was wrong, and I had yet to determine whether I needed it to be my concern again. After all, she owed me, not the other way round.

Isabella had glided into my suburban hair salon some 30 minutes before, with a demure smile on her face. I allowed her to give me a majestically restrained hug and the lightest possible peck on the cheek, not to disturb her immaculate make-up, or my own perfect styling.

For once I felt relieved the afternoon was going slow, and my frumpy assistants, Moira and Beth, were the only ones at the salon. They were barely 18 and horribly impressionable. When they saw Isabella, their mouths agape, they almost stopped breathing. I just raised my index finger behind my daughter's back to silence them, and they sat back down on the sofa. They continued sipping the herbal tea I'd prepared that morning, and they pretended not to be listening in on us. But I knew better.

I turned up the volume on the local radio station to muffle our conversation.

My daughter looked around the salon; she winced when she spotted the door to the backroom, remembering the empty closet. Then she spoke in a weak whisper.

"I hope I am not intruding, mother. May I trouble you for a bun? Pretty please?"

"Sure."

In the routine of my profession, I swivelled around the customers' chair as an invitation to sit. My surprise at seeing Isabella still kept me on my guard.

I scanned my daughter from head to toe, and my gaze

pierced beyond her elegant apparel, but nothing amiss was visible to the naked eye. I bided my time, as I prepared the hair-styling utensils. This was just another hairdo for a well-to-do woman, or so I pretended. I was alert, but my hands remained steady. It was the fear I smelled, fear and something else, a scent in her I didn't recognize. For a moment, Isabella's eyes betrayed a trace of panic, a quiet storm lurking from within, but in a second she blinked it away. Once again, her demure smile was reflected in the mirror.

With each brush stroke, I became more and more annoyed. Not knowing meant not being in control, and I was always in control. I decided to get the ball rolling.

"How is Howard? And the kids?" I asked.

Her neck vein began to pulsate visibly at the mention of her husband. I'd struck a chord. I grinned and wedged some gold hairpins between my lips. I could do hair buns with my eyes closed. I yanked her hair back vigorously, but she didn't complain; she'd grown accustomed to my technique so long ago.

"They are all fine, mother. Thank you."

It didn't sound like it. Her voice was on the verge of its breaking point. I was hoping she hadn't come all this way to do some crying. I despised tears; she'd gotten that from her father's side. I felt her tension, as though a slight breeze would snap her arched back in half, like a twig, but she calmed herself down. Good, at least she'd gotten some dignity from my side of the family.

She seemed cold, yet her skin was hot to the touch. As I placed another pin into her hair, just for a second there, I felt a heat flash scorch my fingertips.

I'd had enough. I was mature enough not to waste my time on curiosity.

Moira and Beth were dying to know what secrets lurked in the lives of the city folk. The little vultures! My family was not a reality show.

"You two, go home. You have the rest of the day off. No wages. Now scoot!"

Frowns crossed their two zit-infested faces, but they left without a word. They knew me well enough to keep their tongues tied.

Hanging the closed sign, I locked the door, pulled down the shutters, and spoke my mind.

"What's going on, girl?"

Before I turned around, my daughter collapsed to the ground. She dragged her body on her elbows to reach the cabinet. There she leaned, her legs just stretched out like those of a mannequin. She seemed as if she was finally ready to say something, but weighing what to say and how, or if she should say anything at all. I was ready to scold her for procrastinating and not telling me what she'd come for, but then something sent me over the edge. Her dress had slid up, revealing the skin on her thigh. *A lady never reveals anything!* I lunged towards her, my hand ready to strike.

"No, mother, stay there," she said in a voice so firm I thought it wasn't hers. "Just *stop...*"

Was that a trace of smoke coming out of her mouth? Maybe fury had made me dizzy, because she'd never said *stop* to me before. How insolent! I took another step closer, but she screamed, "No!"

Now I feared the worst. She'd obviously managed to destroy the only thing she had going for her in life.

"Is Howard leaving you? What on earth have you done?"

She tilted her head and looked at me with a cold glare, her eyes filled with disappointment and accusation. It made her look so indignant and ugly. She started moving on all fours, like a wild cat, her unfinished hair bun resembling a mane. She actually grinned and growled at me, but then spoke quite calmly, enunciating each word with mockery.

"No, mother, Howard is not leaving me. I have always been the modest little wifey you raised me to be. The perfect trophy wife. I cooked and cleaned, and starved myself to look perfect at his conferences and galas. I was back in shape after every birth and never ever spoke out of turn."

Her bitter words spat out at me were too much of a shock for my delicate soul. I took a step back. *Was she blaming ME for something? Must I discipline her again? Where were all these words coming from?* I had to stop this.

But she was relentless. Those eyes glaring at me, almost without blinking. And her skin was changing. *Was it darker, a sparkling bronze shade, or was I in shock?*

"I loved and respected the man you chose for me, through thick and thin. And imagine this - I actually expected my husband to love and respect me back. No, mother, your discipline had not killed the romantic in me, go figure! But he was YOUR choice after all, wasn't he? His claws were bound to show eventually. See, I hadn't really signed up for a mistress or two... or three... or more... Not in our summer villa, our yacht, our bedroom..."

"But how? Who?" I blurted out before I could stop myself.

She looked at her fingernails, thinking. Right before

my eyes, her nails grew into claws. Her talons extended, in slow and steady counterpoint pace to my quickened breathing. *This was only a nightmare, a mirage. I was not really hearing all this, seeing this horror.*

Her eyes suddenly flashed a mad, yellowish spark at me. Then she took a deep breath and her voice restored its calmness.

"How? Easily. Who? My husband, that's who. Oh, you mean, *with whom*? The nanny.... Our pediatrician. My gynaecologist. Nanny number 2. His lawyer. His financier. His colleague's daughter. The local florist girl he used to send me flowers. And..." She looked up, trying to remember and used her fingers to count. Then she shook her head and continued. "No, that's everyone I know about."

"You probably deserved that! Or you just misunderstood something! You were never very bright!" I shouted at her. I wanted her gone.

Did another yellow spark flash from her eyes? Was her hairline receding before my eyes? I needed a drink, fast.

I tried to move, but my legs would not obey. I just leaned on a nearby barstool, hiding weakness from my demented daughter. My head hurt. I closed my eyes, feeling faint. It had never occurred to me that she might have been lying - she had never been very imaginative. How she was even able to put all of this together in full sentences was beyond me.

I regained my composure and decided to send her away, when she suddenly started to chant. The chant was accompanied by a horrible screeching sound, as she carved a heart into the marble floor with her index talon and crossed it out. It was like chalk screeching on a blackboard, but the

talon didn't crumble - the floor did.

This was not happening, she was not here, I was not seeing this...

She gritted her teeth and smacked her lips. She got up, sliding her palms down her body.

"Well, I obviously wasn't very bright," she snorted. Then she took off her stilettos and kicked them under the counter. She looked straight into my eyes, never flinching. "But the marriage you arranged is over."

Why was she doing this to me? After everything I'd done for her, she was implicating me in her problems all over again. I didn't deserve this.

"You don't expect ME to take you back and fix your life again, now do you?" I asked.

She laughed out loud with such open disdain, as if she considered me beneath her. My soul hurt so much that my eyes were playing tricks on me. I slumped back to the ground, exhausted and drained, but another shock followed.

She snarled. Her upper lip raised and revealed her front teeth extending into fangs. Two small, clean, sharp fangs.

I blinked to clear my vision, but the horrifying sight was still there. I closed my eyes, forbidding them to play tricks on me, and pulled my knees to my chin to stop them from shaking.

I'd rely on my other senses; I was a survivor.

"Oh mother, you can forget about all that now," she said with a sigh. "It's old news anyway, from about two years ago."

Two years! How could I not have known?

"But when we came to see the children, you never told ME anything!"

My eyes, firmly shut, allowed me to regain some self-control.

I was supposed to know, I should have been informed. I could have fixed it. Howard wouldn't have divorced her. He would have forgiven her.

"Told YOU? Huh," she rejected my words with scorn. "Actually, I did say something. I told Howard. I threatened to leave him and take the kids with me. You want to know what he did?"

She screamed those last words at me, and the air suddenly smelled of something burnt.

Was she smoking? In my salon? I would not be provoked.

My eyes remained shut, but I listened.

"He punched me, threw me on the bed and injected me with something. I thought it was a rape drug. The following day, I learned it was much more than that. My darling husband, the renowned genetic expert, had been sneaking his experiments out of the lab and into our cellar. He was tampering with it to sell it to the highest bidder."

She had obviously lost her mind, but I was stronger than madness, stronger than she was.

My brain made one more attempt at regaining sanity and control.

"But he was looking for a cure for a deadly virus, wasn't he? That was what he was famous for," I protested.

"Deceit, deceit, more deceit. He was working on a cure and the virus at the same time. He gave me the virus, you see, but somehow - I became the cure. I evolved. And now, I can actually cure diseases, but.... only looking like this."

My mind was on overdrive, running only on fumes,

but she continued to torment me.

"They brought him some new compound from the space lab. He wanted to see what it could do so he used that on me, too. '*A cocktail*,' he said. And I was one of his lab rats! Your daughter - a lab rat!"

Her nearby screams now pierced my ears. The temperature in the room seemed to have risen and I felt sweat dripping from my forehead. *Did she set fire to the place?*

All of a sudden, my left ear burnt, as I heard Isabella whisper directly into it.

"And YOU, mother, you gave me to that man."

I opened my eyes to protest — but froze instead. I faced a monster.

I couldn't even blink. I thought I would never ever be able to close my eyes again.

My daughter's head was completely hairless. Isabella glared at me with yellow eyes. Her skin was smooth, like a beautiful bronze statue, and her clothes were falling off her in scorched rags. Strands of burnt blond hair lay on the floor, still smouldering.

"I thought you'd be happy. You see how special he made me?" Her face was in my face, but then she took a slow step back. "Mind you, I only learned just how special I now am this very morning, so I can understand your shock." She puffed into her rags and they dissipated into ashes. "He said I could never leave him, because I'd die without the drug. And if I did decide to leave, he'd use it on the kids, too."

I was hardly listening to her rant any more.

I needed to act.

I grabbed the barstool behind me and swirled around to defend myself from this unnatural demon questioning my sanity.

Her entire body burst into a torch. Her heat wave sent my poor self flying into the opposite wall. I fell to the floor, struggling to breathe. Blood dripped down my forehead and I tried to wipe it off with my hand, but I could barely raise it for the pain in my broken bones.

I was not going to cry.

I looked up at her, through the dripping crimson veil, and tried to find serenity in voiceless prayer.

"Did that hurt?" she tilted her head in mock baby talk. "I wish I could say I'm sorry."

She sat on the sofa where Moira and Beth had recently been. Like a naked bronze panther, she stretched out her arms and back. Then she elegantly crossed her legs, as if we were having a normal mother-daughter chat, and sat back with a dark, fang-filled smile.

"I know the bar-stool was meant to surprise me, but I don't seem to be taking surprises well these days. In fact, I like to spring them on people. I surprised Howard, too. His experiment took an unexpected turn; my body absorbed the compound and started producing it at will. I no longer needed the drug. Howard realized that just before I did. And then..."

As she leapt to her feet, I crawled backwards to the back room door. In micro-seconds, her eyes became pitch black and her body turned ice-cold and white. My frigid daughter circled around me as if stalking her prey.

"And then..." she roared.

I was petrified. My brain was repeating a mantra –

survive, survive, survive.

If I was meant to hear this story, I would, and then I would wake up from this nightmare, and I would go to confession, and all would be well again.

"He turned to the kids this morning ... He injected them while they were sleeping." She paced the floor now, then stopped and pierced me with her dark-hooded eyes. "The bloody bastard knew my body had changed, but real mother's love would never go away. He knew I'd do anything to keep my kids. When he boasted to me about injecting the kids, I ... I just lost it."

With her last words, her shoulders relaxed, and I watched in shock as she slowly started turning back into her former human self. All I could now hear was my own panicked breathing.

Was it finally over?

Then all hell broke loose. Halfway through the transformation, she suddenly crouched. Again, her body burst into flames, but something different was happening, it was as if lava was melting off her flesh.

I heard myself screaming within my skull.

She rose ... *It* rose straight up, a silhouette of a naked woman's body shaped from lava, not dripping nor seeping, but holding form like a fiery gel. The face was no longer discernible when the erect figure reached its full height. Bare feet stomped and hands shook off sparks, as if shaking off water after a swim. Most of them disappeared, scattered and cooled into dust under the furniture.

Just a single spark reached my left foot; it burnt a hole through my slipper and penetrated my flesh before cooling down.

"Oh..." she said, and chuckled, shrugging her shoulders in feigned apology.

Her face reappeared, features again recognizable, as her lava body cooled down. Once again, her figure turned back into bronze. Her eyes glowed yellow, and her mouth opened into a fang-filled smile. Light came out of her mouth, before words filled it.

"As you can see, Howard's pet project backfired. Kind of like yours, mother. Meet the new me." She spread her arms wide, proudly displaying her morbid state as she performed a grotesque curtsey.

"But... you... the kids... Are they alive?" I whispered.

"Of course they are, mother. I can control my power when I want to!" she yelled at me, changing composition from bronze into ice with every step she made. "I am not a monster!"

Then she stopped and gazed at her reflection in the mirror. She grinned. "Oh well, I can see your point. But the kids are okay now, back at school. And I am fine now, thank you for asking. Well, some side effects, as you can see," she bowed in self-irony, "but okay. We are all A-Okay now." Her voice became eerie and cold. "Except Howard."

"Howard?"

She grinned her sharp fangs at me like a raging beast, and then growled, as she leaned her face in close to mine, "Your precious Howard wanted a fiery woman. So I gave him fire - this dragon lady in full form. He should have known never to touch this dragon's jewels - my kids! Never! And never more!"

"What have you done?"

Her sparks glistened in my eyes, blinding me.

"Oh, don't worry, mother, he simply melted in my embrace. Melted, I tell you. Doctor's signet ring, his wedding ring, teeth and all. Shame about the bed though. And such a pity he's going to miss the charity gala tonight."

Her laughter was bitter and fearless.

I was prepared to beg for my own life.

"Now what?" I asked.

She smiled, moved her hands down her bronze chest as if to shake off some dust, and then stretched her arms above her head and sighed with content.

"Oh, I feel so much better now that I've told you."

As she strolled back to the customer chair, her bronze form returned to its normal, human state. Her claws withdrew, her face took back its shape, and her eyes assumed their natural colour. As Isabella sat down, she turned towards the mirror and beckoned me, with a hair brush in her hand.

"Come, mother, do my hair for me."

My breath caught for a second as I watched new hair grow from her head, like snakes slithering out of their lair.

I thought I wouldn't be able to move, but somehow I did. Her beckoning hand issued an invisible energy surge which guided my body, zombie-like, towards her. My underwear was wet and I smelled rancid like a stray cat.

When I reached the chair, by habit, my hand seized the hair brush. The golden tresses of her hair glistened before me as if nothing had happened.

"On second thought, mother, just leave my hair down. We'd never find the pins again, anyway."

Isabella rose, naked and proud, and walked over to the clothes hanger on the wall. She grabbed a raincoat someone

had forgotten, and tied the belt. Isabella stepped into her discarded stilettos, like a little girl with a new pair of dancing shoes. Then, with a princess-like smile, she spoke to me.

"I really must borrow this; I feel a bit exposed. And we wouldn't want anyone to know just how special I really am, now would we? I may be a desperate widow, but I am still Mrs. Deceit."

The salon door closed behind her without a sound.

I dropped everything to the floor with a clatter. I had to reach the back room. The closet door was easy to unlatch. All I had to do was throw out all the dirty towels. I held my breath as I crawled into the emptied closet, and shut the door. I sat on the floor, holding my knees tight to my chin, and whispered to myself.

"Keep quiet and you'll be safe. Keep quiet and you'll be safe. Keep quiet and you'll be safe..."

© ANITA KOVACEVIC 2016. ALL RIGHTS RESERVED.

+++

9

UBIQUITOUS

Geoff Nelder

London, Winter 2100 AD

Oblivion is a few minutes away, yet sitting in this sordid café you wouldn't think it. Thousands of years developing civilization and we can be snuffed over monetary problems. The exuberant Zia helps. I swapped partners last month because I thought she'd take my plight seriously. She does, but only to amuse herself. Maybe I'm wrong. She might be the one I need to sort my woes and keep me alive and sane.

This busy sordid snackerie with its cream, dirty walls tries to hide me in vain. I must concentrate – she's mid-sentence already...

"...they only scare the shit out of their victims, right?"

A knock at the greasy window behind me gives me tachycardiac twitches. A damn kid with a stick. I wave him

away while assuring my heart they've not arrived. Every shadow flitting across the walls of this instant dyspepsia emporium fists my hands.

"I heard they cut a debtor's trigger finger off, then made him eat it so it couldn't be sown back on." I say this but know Zia is in denial.

"It's just a story, Tedrig. Be a good idea to change your name, by the way. What's the point in being nervous?" says Zia between sipping her liquidized lunch. My nose wrinkles at the aroma of synthetic carrotberry. It's deliberate. She knows my olfactories do overtime when I'm stressed.

"You're right, Zia, they're coming for me any time. Are you sure we haven't enough?"

She checks her iPad. "Three K more than ten minutes ago."

"Send it them, maybe they'll call off the goons."

"No. I'll invest in QuickProf again. How much are they blackmailing you?"

"Four mill. Let's move to that corner table with our backs to the wall. We can watch the window and door."

"No."

The word rattles around in my head. Why did I have to fall for such a bitch? I must get a buzz from being needled – I had no idea.

"I don't like being crept up on. Stay here if you want." But she dawdles after me. She specialises in leading from behind.

"Your fault."

"What? Siphoning off the rounded-down remainders of thirty million salaries into a dummy account? Yeah, I suppose it was slightly illegal."

"No, dummy. Being caught by pimply teen hackers who traced you."

"I offered them a share."

"Different generation. They made more selling you to the syndicate. What will they look like?"

I don't answer. No one can tell me how the enforcers of the syndicate appear. SentientWeb has all the info of the planet except that. I haven't smiled for days, and I've a reputation for laughing in the face of danger to maintain, but how does danger sneer today? The aircon fails to stem the cascade of stinging perspiration. Shame, because I need perfect vision as my eyes nictate between shadows. Greed plunged me into this mess, but the greed of others has secured my fate. If only those quantum physics promises of simultaneous existences would manifest themselves. Just one parallel otherness would be so handy.

I watch as Zia dabs at her wrist iPad conjuring up more credits, but what if there isn't enough when…

A crash in the kitchen jerks me up on my feet but I crumple into my chair when my legs refuse to behave.

Zia laughs at my jitters. Maybe false bravado? "It's only a kitchen auto-slave dropping plates. What a pansy."

The word 'pansy' hovers between us, teasing. I will it away while glancing behind at the kitchen swing door wondering if I should change seats again.

"Fear will kill you," Zia says, while picking at her edible drink container, popping chunks in her mouth.

She's right. I haven't plumbed these depths of despair before. I don't do morbid. Not until now.

"Go on, Tedrig, slip away if you can make your legs work."

"Where to?"

"Where SentientWeb can't locate you."

"I'm not spending the rest of my life in a submarine."

"There's cabins in the mountains with no SW."

"It doesn't need to be linked. This watch, our ID-bankcards, and intra-skull well-being monitors all have microchips that can be pinged. And I'm not going to build a Faraday Cage around an ancient miner's shack in the Blue Mountains. I could keep moving, but that's no life."

"I'm not stupid."

"Then you know I've no choice. What's the worst that can happen?"

"They could ask for all the money you scammed – the whole eight mill. Let's see. Yea, you now have half that."

"Send it to them."

"Too late, the deadline passed ten seconds ago, which means they'll want all eight, which you frittered away..."

I drum nervous fingers on the plasi-tabletop. I should know better than to allow fidgeting of my own digits especially while looking elsewhere when others might be watching.

"Idiot, you've just ordered five tofu pizzas. Tap the cancel square. Too late, it's charged your account. Now you have eighty four fewer credits."

"You should get away from me, Zia."

"What? And miss the show?" She tosses her vermilion hair in mock shock. It's an effective gesture since everyone else has the silver-coated bald head look, including me. I try to be inconspicuous, which is another ironic twist in me choosing her for a swap-mate.

I attempt shock with, "Stay then but don't develop apoplexy when they take you instead of me in lieu of the

money. And it won't be any use gooey-eyeing sexual emanations, they'd need to sell your body parts to recover the debt and as a lesson to others."

"Nice try, Tedrig. They'll know we're not that close – four hundred creds maybe, but not four mill. No, they'll snip off one of your fingers, and again for each day you fail to pay up."

Instinctively I sniff my index finger. Tomato sauce. I don't remember... getting back to now I say, "You've been watching too many ancient gangster movies. My med insurance covers replacement fingers."

She sniggers. "I bet you've subcutaneous morphine blisters ready to pop."

"Of course." Nevertheless a shiver devil dances in my spine at the thought of my digits being secateured. I shut my eyes and listen to my pulse doing the rumba. "Zia, that's why it's better for you to sneak away before they hostage you."

"Too late, three heavies are crowding the door. Come on, out the back."

In spite of logic, I follow her into the kitchen – a set of auto-microwave shelf units. Rats suck up floored, steaming red bolognaise. Ah, Zia crashes at the rear exit, I pull at her sleeve.

"They'll have someone there."

"No, they'll assume you won't run 'cos there's no point."

Cold air arrests us for a moment before we run across the alley into GameHeaven. Comfortingly dark although it's musty. I pull her into a sensory booth. My worry makes me stroke my shiny head. Silver dandruff floats, like anti-missile

chaff, to the games console.

"Madness. They'll know we're here."

"Maybe not, it's too close to the café for their one-metre GPS to be totally accurate. Reflections distort—"

"Forget applied physics, this place will have pinged my credit chip already. I'm surrendering. There's no sanctuary - I want to finish it now. There's no need for you to be implicated. It's been a blast knowing you."

"You wimp. OK, I'm coming too."

Anxious but less terrified with the decision made, I stride back into the café from the kitchen to confront the heavies. Zia pushes into me from behind when my feet emergency brake. The three black-suited men with mirror-eyes sit at a table sipping rhubarb crush through jumbo straws indenting their cheeks.

"They don't look so heavy," Zia says.

"It's not them." Sighing with relief yet knowing nothing is over, I settle into our lookout corner to wait for the real syndicate collectors. "I'll order two cafeinees while you check my balance."

"Yeah, there's no point being nervous."

Five minutes drag like hours. A black ant traversing the table stops to look at me with pity.

"He's back," Zia says, forcing my eyes from the ant, wondering if it's a syndicate micro spy. The kid pulls faces at the window before tapping the window again. Attention gained he pulls a finger across his throat. I choose to mock laugh at his impudence then wonder if he knows...

"Look at that, Tedrig."

"I am. Damn kid."

"No. Look at the others – hilarious."

I laugh at grim reality to endure it. She laughs at me. But I glance and she's right. All the customers are staring at the kid as if he's putting on a bizarre show for them, unaware that he targets me. I start to finger him but delete the retribution. Aren't I the adult?

A thought stutters. "Do you think—"

"Sure. He's one of the hackers. So that's what a midget nerd looks like."

"Zia, carefully sneak out your phone and snap him. I've an idea."

The kid's freckled face transforms from scorn to shock when the flash greets him. It's my turn, I wonder if he... Yes, he's a runt but he's smart. Sufficiently savvy to know events have switched. He drops his stick along with his bravado. He doesn't know what to do. Looks up and down the street doing my looking-out for the heavies. I bet he wishes witnessing my torment wasn't on his fun-things-to-do today. He'll come in.

"I've uploaded the snap – get your phone ready to record under the table."

I'd already done that but if Zia thought of it, the kid might. Or he'll have a jammer. I do it anyway but on my belt. The door lets him shuffle in and over to us.

Awkward silence thickens between us until the kid slices through it. "Don't like me picture taken."

I shrug, Zia laughs. Bad habit in front of the wronged.

His freckles play join the dots as he snarls, "Gimme the cam."

"Or what?" I say, feeling I have an embryonic plan gurgling up.

"I make it worse for you. I'll send everything to Data Cops."

"How can it be worse? The syndicate you set on me is about to take all my credits, assets and probably demand my bodily parts for instant organ sales." It would be comic if it wasn't true.

Zia leans towards him jabbing a straw. "You're really worried, kid. That image is going to identify you isn't it? You've wronged bigger than this and it can be linked?"

His face tells us she's right. OK, I robbed millions, but who notices their pay is missing 0.1 credit of their monthly salary of a hundred thousand? This monkey's probably ripped off bigger. I give it a shot.

"Big corps or the military?"

His face pales bringing his freckles into dark relief.

"Kid, how old are you?" Zia asks. She looks maternal - it doesn't suit her.

"Twelve, why?"

I butt in. "Grief, kid, and I bet you're richer than me. Planning to retire at sixteen?"

At last a toothy grin. He whips out his phone, utters a password followed by: "Nine." Or was it: "Nein." He looks at Zia, then me. "Nearly pulled it off, didn't I?"

I watch him pick up his stick as he leaves. He taps the window. I kinda wave.

"It's over," says Zia, worrying her iPad. "The Syndicate kept four mill for their trouble, but that's it. Finished."

Fate's given me a hand. It could've been bad if the kid had another year or two in him, taking him beyond stick tapping.

"Tedrig. I feel the need to be fed and waited on by real

people. Let's go to RealEats, and there's really no point being nervous now."

"I'm not. Zia, thanks for your invaluable and digit-rescuing tactics, but..."

"You'd rather eat somewhere else?"

"Yes, somewhere different to where you..."

"Actually, I think we're through. Sorry, Tedrig but you're too nice for me. Hey, you're dumping *me* aren't you? OK, I'll see you an estimate of my quota of your gains plus a keep-quiet bonus. Yes? Good luck at the next partner swap."

She purses those full lips and blows me a kiss as she scuttles out. I blow back. Damn, I'll have to choose another partner. I'm getting nervous again.

© Geoff Nelder 2016. All rights reserved.

+++

10

KEEPING IT IN THE FAMILY

Traci Sanders

The sound of shoes scuffing against the marble hospital floor pulls me from my magazine. I've been in this confining hospital bed staring at these depressing gray walls for what seems like forever, but it's only been a few weeks ... since the accident.

My husband Sam approaches my bed and runs a finger along my cheek. His hazel eyes show exhaustion and worry, as if he hasn't slept in years. "Hi, honey. How are you today?"

Here we go. "I'm fine, um..."

"Sam. My name is Sam. I'm your husband. You still don't remember me?"

I look down and twist my wedding band nervously. His voice is sweet and inviting, so much emotion—deeper and stronger than I've ever experienced from him. He is usually such a boring person, showing no passion about

anything, even me. Our bedroom life has been little more than a series of disappointments, when he's not too tired, of course. Who the hell would want to go back home to that? This is my escape. Thank God for that hit I took to the head in the car accident. It was just what I needed—a blow just hard enough to knock some sense into me, and fool everyone into thinking I have amnesia. *The perfect escape.*

"Honey, you have to remember. I'm your husband. I'm here to take you home."

"I'm sorry. I just don't remember you. I can't go home with a stranger. I just can't," I tell him, turning on the waterworks now and my breath coming in short. This warrants sympathy from the good doctor who is just entering my room.

"I'm sorry, Mr. Martin. I can't have you upsetting my patient. I know this is hard for you, but I'm going to have to ask you to leave so I can consult with Kelly to find out what we need to do from here."

Sam looks back at me and runs his fingers through his dark brown hair in frustration and then finally steps into the hallway. *Thank God we don't have kids for him to be able to pull that card on me.*

"Thank you, Doctor Wills. I'm just so scared. I don't know what to do. I can't go home with a strange man. I just can't."

The fifty-something-year-old doctor covers my hand with his and smiles at me with his dark brown, teddy bear eyes. "Calm down, Kelly. We'll figure this all out somehow. But we have to discharge you today. Other than your memory loss, you have no medical reason to stay here. It's hospital policy. Is there a family member we can call? Do

you remember *anyone?*"

I look down at my lap. "I... I don't know."

"It's okay. We'll see what we can come up with."

I watch his tanned, athletic frame exit the room, and when the door opens I see Sam pacing back and forth in the hallway. He looks back at me with desperate eyes. He's kind of cute in his worn-out jeans and gray hoodie, not his typical suit and tie.

I sit up in bed as the door closes again and Sam remains in the hallway, greeting a woman. *Is that, Lori, my half-sister?* She embraces Sam and kisses him on the cheek. They are standing close enough to touch—all body parts, it seems. Lori and I haven't spoken in months and she's definitely not a person who'd be on my emergency contact list. *What the hell is she doing here?*

Next, I see the person I've been waiting for—Patrick—Sam's older brother, the Martin man I *should have* married. He's a fireman, not a boring accountant. He has these striking blue eyes and taut abs. I just want to lick each one of them. He was already married when Sam and I started dating, so I figured I'd lost my chance. But he got a divorce a few months ago. Now he's a free man. And soon, I'll be a free woman. I'll have a legitimate reason to divorce Sam and then I'll make my move on Patrick.

I continue to flip through my magazine, pretending not to watch Sam and Lori and Patrick all interact ... and hug, and... *why is Lori kissing Patrick? On the lips! What the hell is going on here?*

My blood boils and heat rises in my face. I flip through my magazine even faster, not looking at a single page. I can hear their muffled voices outside the door and I

see Lori's hand wrapped lovingly around Patrick's. He tucks a stray blond curl behind her ear and she uncrosses her tanned leg away from Sam and re-crosses it toward Patrick, leaning in to him with a tight little black dress barely covering her five-feet-four cheerleader frame.

They all three get up and walk toward my door. I inhale a sharp breath and brace myself for the charade, just a little longer.

"Hi, honey. Your sister is here to see you. The doctor said you can stay with her until your memory returns. I know you two haven't always seen eye to eye but there is no one else we could call. Since your parents are—"

Dead. I know, I think to myself.

"Hey, sis," she says in a voice that would proclaim no bad blood between us.

I bite my lip and narrow my eyes at her.

"And do you remember my brother, Patrick?" Sam adds.

Only every night in my dreams, I say in my head.

Lori smiles at me and moves closer to Patrick, as if to stake her claim, like she's done so many times before ... with every guy I've ever shown an interest in.

Sam continues, "It's the craziest thing. Lori and Patrick met at the attorney's office where he got his divorce. They've been practically inseparable ever since."

"Do you remember me, sweetie?" Lori asks, playing the concerned sister role to the letter.

Yeah, I remember you, you lying, backstabbing bitch. The sister I never wanted. The sister who stole my family from me. The one my parents loved even more than me, their own flesh and blood.

"I... I'm... sorry. I just don't remember," I say, lying too easily.

"Well, I'm going to let you come stay with me for a while and we'll work on that," she says with a chuckle, and grabs my hand in a supportive-sister way.

"No, I don't think—"

"—You can take the guest room. Patrick's been sleeping over on occasion, but I'm sure we can find somewhere else for him to crash," she says with a smirk. I catch a knowing glance between the two of them.

"Okay. I suppose," I say with a slight nod, still playing the amnesia card.

Sam smiles and covers my hand with his. "That's great, honey. You can spend some quality time with your sister until your memory comes back."

"Yeah," I say slowly.

"Would you guys excuse me? I'd like to have a sisterly chat with Kelly," Lori says to the men, and flashes a charming smile.

Sam kisses my hand and walks out the door with Patrick. My heart skips a beat as Lori stands beside my bed, staring me down. Then she leans in close and whispers through a tight voice, "I know you remember me. I'm on to your little game, sis."

I inhale sharply and ask, "What the hell are you doing here?"

"Didn't you know? Sam called me when the accident happened. Yeah, I've been taking care of him and your house since you've been laid up in this bed. He's been quite happy to have me around, taking care of his *needs.*"

"You wouldn't," I say through gritted teeth.

She purses her lips, licks her teeth and says in a smug voice, "A lonely man will do some crazy things, you know." She takes a glance around the room, then inhales and exhales audibly as she straightens my bed cover. "You might think he's boring, but there's a tiger underneath that suit and tie. They can all be tigers with the right trainer. You just don't know how to handle a man. You never did," she says with a snicker.

I grip the covers on my bed and almost yell in a hushed voice, "Why do you hate me? What did I ever do to you?"

"Like you don't know, little *sister*," she replies, anger lacing her voice. "You had all the friends in school, all the cool boyfriends with cars, you were invited to all the cool parties, and you had a real family."

"A family who seemed to love you more than me," I cut in quickly.

"Really? Are you kidding me?"

"Mom took you shopping all the time, without me. Dad spent hours and hours with you, teaching you how to do this or that. All of that time, spent on *you,* not their *real* daughter."

She nods her head and pulls her lips together in a sarcastic pout. "Sure, they spent time with me ... telling me how I should be more like *you!* I should study harder like you. I should learn to drive like you. You, you, you! It was always about you. They never wanted another daughter. They already had the *perfect one.* Not that you deserved them. You never appreciated them. Then you go off and get married, to the perfect guy, and you don't even realize what you have, once again."

"What business of yours is it how I treat my parents or my husband? It's *my* life!" I reply in a louder whisper.

She narrows her eyes at me. "Not anymore, dear sister. It's my life now. I'm taking everything you've got, everything you care about."

My heart races and my mind is flooded with thoughts. *What do I do? Do I fight for Sam? He's a good guy. I know he'd never cheat on me if it wasn't for this evil bitch and her seductive ways. He'd have to be drunk or something. Do I keep up the charade and go for Patrick?* Then it dawns on me. "If you want Sam and you know I like Patrick, why don't you just take Sam and leave Patrick alone?"

She offers a sinister laugh. "Ha! You'd love that, wouldn't you? I've known you've had the hots for that fireman for a long time now, neglecting your poor husband to fantasize about his brother. You're despicable. You still don't know how to appreciate a good thing."

"Nothing has happened between us. I've never cheated on Sam," I say in a matter-of-fact voice. "So what do you want with Patrick anyway?"

"Oh, he's just for fun. Let me tell you. He is one sexy fireman who knows how to use that hose," she says with an evil smile plastered on her perfectly made-up face.

It takes everything I have to keep from punching her. But I can't let on to anyone that I know her that well. Sam and Patrick have peeked through the glass a few times, checking on us. So I keep my composure as well as I can.

"So, I've signed the papers and you'll be coming home with me, where I can keep an eye on you until your memory returns."

I bite the inside of my cheek. *I'm screwed. What now?*

Sam knocks on the door as he opens it a bit. "You two okay in here?" he says with a smile. Suddenly, I'm lost in his eyes, his beautiful hazel eyes that I fell in love with so long ago, the same eyes that were focused on nothing but me the whole time I was walking down the aisle toward him at our wedding. *He's a good man. He loves me.* And to my surprise, I'm filled with warm memories and affection ... no... attraction toward this man, unlike any I've ever known before.

Sam asks again, "Hello, ladies? Is everything okay here?"

I look at Lori; she's playing the concerned sister role again. I narrow my eyes at her and say, "We're fine, Sam, just having a sisterly chat. But I'm exhausted, honey. Can we go home now?"

"What? Kelly, you want to go *home?* Our home? You remember me?"

"Of course I remember you, silly. You're my husband." I cut my eyes at Lori as I pull him close to kiss him. Even though I didn't throw emphasis audibly on the word "my" I know she gets the message because she slants her eyes at me and bites her lip. I decide to throw out the innocent victim card. "Why are you all looking at me so funny?"

Sam covers my hand with his and a tear threatens to roll down his cheek. "Kelly, you had a head concussion and it caused you to have amnesia. You didn't remember anyone ... until now," he says with a chuckle that's infused with relief and joy.

"Wow, Sam, I'm so sorry. That must have been horrible for you. But don't worry, honey. I'm fine now, and I want to go home—our home, with you." I offer a genuine

smile and kiss him once more. He hugs me tight and when our bodies touch, I feel a heat rise up in me that I've never experienced before.

Lori is speechless. I know she wants to protest all of this, but there is nothing she can say without exposing her secrets too. Then she narrows her eyes at me and pulls Patrick close as if to say, *"At least I still have the hot fireman."*

I smile back, though she doesn't know why ... yet.

Sam wipes the tears from his eyes and says, "Well, let me check with the doctor to let him know what's going on and we'll get you out of here. Patrick, want to walk with me?"

Patrick smiles. "Sure, bro. Be right back, Lori. Good to have you back, Kelly."

Lori smiles at him and waits for the door to close. Then she whips around to face me. "All right, what the hell is going on? Just what kind of game are you playing here?"

"Oh nothing. I just realized how much I love Sam. It's like I'd *forgotten* for a while somehow," I say with a wry smile.

"You don't love him. You just don't want *me* to have him. Guess I'll have to settle for Patrick, the luscious fireman," she says, trying to rile me up.

"Yeah, for some reason he doesn't seem all that appealing to me anymore. I guess I just needed to be reminded that I already have the *right* Martin brother." *Game on, sister.*

"You may think that now, dear sister, but there's something else I haven't told you yet. Something that's going to turn your little plan upside down."

"And what's that?" I ask, forcing a smile to hide the nervousness in my voice.

She leans in close to my ear and shivers surge through my body at her words. "I'm pregnant."

© *Traci Sanders 2016. All rights reserved.*

+++

11

SET FOR SATURDAY

Keith Dixon

He'd do it this weekend. Definitely. Had to be done. Sorted.

He unclips the safety belt and climbs out of the mini. Racing green. Cooper edition. Alloy wheels. Union Jack roof. Goes with his image—flash all right, but respectful of tradition. You don't forget your roots. What have you got left if you haven't got roots?

Locking the car, he straightens his tie, checks his hair in the reflection from the windows—gelled perfection—spins cockily on a heel and pushes stiff-armed into the pub.

From light to dark. Quiet this time of day. Everyone at work earning a crust. More fool them. Couple of midday boozers. Group of pensioners in the corner, carefully sawing through pork escalope in a Dijonnais sauce. Smell of dirty socks. Jackie Davis smoking a fag and tapping the ash on the floor because he doesn't care, never has done, never will.

"Jackie."

"Des."

Out through the back. Light again. A conservatory with five wooden tables. Big glass windows looking over the canal. Billy sitting at the one nearest the lawn, shuffling a beer mat end over end. Stubby fingers. Hair looking greasy, sticking to his forehead. Spots on his chin and working up round his nose, the juicy hollows at the top of his nostrils. Doesn't look well, all told. But he's the one to talk to. Keep him sweet.

"Billy."

"Des."

He sits opposite Billy and lights up. Big breath in and the smoke soothes him. Reaches over and takes a swig from Billy's drink. Some vile muck. Puts the glass down carefully.

"You sorted for this weekend?" Billy says. Not a question—a push, a poke in the chest.

"What's to sort? We're in, we're out." Hates justifying himself to Billy. Makes him feel not right. Like he was a kid.

"Celebrations and what not," Billy says. "Fireworks. People out and about. Especially that early."

"I've said it's all right, it's all right. And I've told you—it's got to be early."

Billy's not watching him. "Your first time."

"Yeah, and?"

"I put you in for this." Billy stops turning the beer mat. There's a threat coming. "It's gotta go right."

"You don't look well, do you know that?"

Billy still looks away. "Don't be such a kid."

Feels hot here all of a sudden. He wants to go but that would be worse than staying. He needs to breathe—Carol told him that. When you have attacks you need to breathe. Oxygen helps.

Billy's looking at him now. Black eyes you can't see into. Not trusting.

"What's happening with that woman?" he says.

"It's sorted."

"Already? You were waiting for a good time to tell her, you said."

"This Saturday night. After."

"You don't need a woman. She knows what you do it mucks things up."

"She doesn't know."

"Yet. What'll she do when you ditch her?"

He doesn't know. He can't tell. He's been lying to her so it's easier to dump her. Easier on who?

He says, "I don't care."

Billy's still looking at him.

Across the road, he hears the glass break. Winds up the car window—keep the cold out. A light goes on in the back of the shop. So he's in now. Lifting the boxes out the back window. Call that security. Flat screen TVs are best—light to carry, slim boxes. Ready market round the estate, no questions asked.

He sees Carol in his head. In her room. All pale green. Posters on the wall—Brad Pitt. Johnny Depp. She likes Yanks. Brushing her hair. Keeps it strong, she says. Now dabbing something on her eyelids. Some colour. Leaning in at a mirror with her mouth open like they do. He'll see her in a while and tell her and that'll be it. Sorted. Won't have to keep thinking about her then.

Not worrying—thinking. There's a difference.

Just because he's seen her a couple of times doesn't

mean he's got the bug. Like them other men she's been with. Keep calling her up and making her laugh. Switching off the phone and looking at him, saying, "What? What—I'm supposed to stop them calling me up? How am I supposed to do that, then?" And laughing. Like it wasn't important. Keeping him guessing, off his balance.

Then suddenly there's two police cars parking up in front of the shop. He winds down the window. Hears a voice—a shout like a bark. The light in the shop goes out. There's three policemen—no, four. They're running. He hears feet. And something knocks over. Crashes over. Suddenly everything sounds loud. Like everyone's listening, and watching. Phones with cameras pointing out of bedroom windows.

And he sees Billy running. Knows it's him. The long arms in silhouette. Something about how the legs work from the waist down. There's two policemen chasing after. Holding on to their hats like people in a film.

Start the engine. Start the sodding engine. Billy's gone behind a building. Can't hear anything now because the engine's started. And the radio booms on till he stabs a finger and pushes it off. Winds down the window again to listen.

Wait ... Wait ... He'll be doubling back. Billy planned this. He walked round the area yesterday afternoon. He took notes. He's cool, so wait. He'll come round the back, watching the cops, opening the rear door when they're not looking, diving in and breathing hard. Telling him to go go go. Any minute.

One of the police cars kicks off its roof light. For a split second he thinks it's fireworks. All that blue light.

Swinging round and bouncing off the inside of the cabin. He swallows his heart and winds up the window and drives off.

Billy can look after himself.

It's still early for a Saturday. Driving around in lots of traffic. All these lights. Watch out for police. Up and down streets, turn corners slowly. Be careful. Don't attract attention. Up through the gears and down again, thinking ahead, watch out for cars and take your time.

Out of the city now, into country lanes. Sky like black velvet. No lights except a big yellow moon. His heart's beating normal though his breathing's still weird. Push it down, swallow it. Act normal because you are normal. You're normal like everyone else. Breathe in. Oxygen helps.

There's the place—big place, with car parking in front. Big hotel. Bit posh. Lots of windows with lights on. Some kind of dance music bouncing into the night. He can see shadows inside, jumping up and spreading across the walls like paint. He can smell the fireworks already, pulled into the car through the heating ducts. Smell of cordite. Wonders if it's like this in a gunfight. You smell more than you see. But fireworks are going off. Show must have started. Didn't wait for him, did they? Not with paying customers to deal with.

Turns off the engine and sits and watches some rockets go off. Couple of bangers make the air throb. Light appearing from everywhere. Inside of the car showing white, like a hospital. Makes him think: Get out. Get out the car.

Slams the door and leans against it. Legs feeling funny. Trembling. Breathe again, deep breaths. He looks up and sees an

umbrella of light open up. Then another—red, this one. More whiz-bangs shooting up with a crackle, then a pause, then a deep sharp boom like a door slamming in heaven.

Feels like he's being taken out of himself. Doesn't have to think any more. Just sit back and let everything else happen. Like being hit about the head. Colour and sound wash over him. Leans back against the car and watches through half-shut eyes. Everyone else is out there now. And the world is loud and full of red and blue and gold. And god it's not what he expected. Not even what he wanted. He wanted it to be hard and sharp and he wanted it to hurt when he turned and banged against it. But not to hurt like this. Like it was real.

Breathing settled now. Just watching the lights. Find Carol in a minute.

He becomes aware of the crowd. Four deep round a stack of burning stuff. Faces upturned like pennies. Feels good. It's all right. They didn't catch him. He wants to laugh now. Feels his mouth pulling back, lips wide. Big smile for the sky. All that colour banging up there. There's a word he can't say. Looks pretty. Doesn't use that word. Pretty. That's a feeling.

Then a whiz and a whoosh and another bang down here. The crowd talking and laughing. All these strangers. They don't know what he knows. Not been there, have they? No right to know. Why should they? That's why he's different.

Time to tell Carol now. Go find her. He pushes himself upright and leans into the wind. Skirts the crowd, on the edge, feeling comfortable. They don't see him because he doesn't want them to.

Sees her—there, with her mates. Long coats they wear. Her dark hair like a curtain swishes this way, that. Touches her on the shoulder. Watches her surprise as she turns. Finds the words in his mouth but they don't taste good. Just looks at her. Her round face. Oval eyes, laughing.

She's saying something. It's like her eyes are saying it too. Can't hear for the bangs. Noises overhead. All around. Colour and noise and her mouth's moving. Her eyes watching his. And he feels something like a pliers squeezing the top of his nose. A tightness that hurts. And the words won't come while he's still looking at her. And he's thinking of Billy running. His legs the way they move. And Carol's still talking but it's too loud and now he can feel something hot in his eyes. Probably the bonfire making them run. But he can feel a tightening and squeezing and it's pulling his mouth down, so that he can't speak, and the heat in his eyes seems fluid, like it's moving and he looks again at Carol.

She's stopped talking and is watching him, watching him catch his breath, and blink his eyes and stare and stare at her, while the water in his eyes becomes too much and tips and runs over his lids and then runs hotly down his cheeks, so that he's embarrassed.

Turns away, walks away. Fuck that. He can rob a shop and leave a mate but he can't lie to a woman.

Some things he won't do.

© KEITH DIXON 2016. ALL RIGHTS RESERVED.

+++

12

COLD

Lubna Sengul

They say that revenge is a dish best served cold. Oh, it was cold all right, everything was cold to touch. Not just cold, but the kind of icy cold that gets right beneath your skin and into your bones—making them shudder all on their own, and no matter how much you try to warm yourself the cold won't leave. The kind of cold where your cold breath meets cold air and actual solid ice begins forming.

It took me a while to understand what had happened as I looked at myself lying alone in the woodlands. I mean, how was it possible that I could see myself asleep on the floor? At first I thought I'd stumbled across someone who just looked like me, but then I noticed *it*. The gaping gash to the head, the one, which my supposedly loving dear Mummy had given me. Oh yes, that was the day I discovered that I, Sarah May, was no longer a living human being. But I was alive in a different way, for I could still see and hear everything in this world just as before, except it seemed that no one could see me—well, that is what I first

thought.

Even though home was a scary thought, it was also the only place that I knew. I found my way back there, and watched Mummy with her horrible new boyfriend tell the police that I was missing.

"I'm not missing, I'm right here." I said, waving my arms. The police ignored me and so did Mummy's boyfriend.

But not Mummy, she gave me a cold pale stare. "How?" she mumbled.

"Sorry?" questioned the Police.

"Oh, nothing," she mumbled again, without removing her eyes away from me.

It then dawned on me that karma had played a major part in this. I had been sent to remind Mummy about her wicked deeds.

She wasn't always a bad Mummy, although distant she used to be nice enough to make sure I was fed and clothed, and if I was lucky, every now again she'd cuddle me. But around my eighth birthday she met Jack. Oh I hated him, and he knew it too as I refused to listen to him. So he often threatened to break up with Mummy. Many times Mummy told me off and demanded that I behave. I was grounded so regularly that eventually I became used to being sent to bed without dinner—just so she could spend time with Jack, and show him that she was listening to him.

One day I told Mummy and Jack exactly what I thought. He demanded that I'd be punished and that's what Mummy did, she hit me on the head with a high heeled shoe. I don't think she meant to kill me, but killed me she did. She thought so little of me that she dumped my little

body, alone in the woods, where the cold seeped in.

"Mummy are you happy now?" I would ask her, but she always ignored me.

"Why did you hurt me Mummy?" I would ask and again she'd ignore me. It hurt that she wouldn't even look at me. She just kept herself busy with that horrid Jack.

"What do you like about Jack? He is horrid!" I saw Mummy's fists clenching and the way she stared at me, as if she was going to punish me again. That was it. Jack was the trigger, the way to get her to listen to me. So I played on that as often as I could—especially whenever he was around.

"Jack is boring," I would repeatedly say.

Eventually, Mummy would lose her patience and yell back at me. "Go away! You're not real!"

"Who ya talkin to luv?" Jack asked

"'It's her, Sarah. Can't you see her?"

"She ain't here, luv. It's all up there," said Jack, motioning his finger to his head. At first, he seemed fine with Mummy saying she had the feeling that I was there with them, but after a few days, it started to bother him.

"Will you give it a rest, Martha, for god's sake you sound like 'em people who belong in the loony bin!" Jack said as he sipped on his beer.

"What else am I supposed to do? She's always bloody here, won't let me sleep, goes everywhere I go, I hear her constantly taunting me," Mummy said.

"Well you'd betta do sumfing about it, luv, it's getting a bit weird."

I laughed out aloud so that only Mummy could hear me. "You hurt me for someone who thinks you're weird," I said.

"Shut up," Mummy said.

"Don't tell me to shut up," Jack replied, thinking Mummy was speaking to him. "You're lucky to have me sticking by ya after what you done."

"I did it because of you!" Mummy screamed at him.

"Er nah, she was outta control. Must've have got that from you," Jack said, and got up to leave. "I ain't putting up with ya anymore, plus I have someone else now."

Mummy cried for days after Jack left. She tried to call him so many times, and every time he ignored her. She cried more for losing him then she did for hurting me.

"You wanted me gone for him and now he has left you," I whispered to her.

"Why are you doing this? This all of your fault," she would shout. No remorse for losing her child. Only that Jack had left her. She felt nothing for the life that she took and that it was my life.

On the night she killed me she was listening to *Bleeding Love* by Leona Lewis, so I made sure I sang it every night to her so she couldn't sleep. It was driving her mad.

"Fine I'll do it. I'll confess, please just leave me alone now," she said one morning, and then she called the police. At last, after forty days my body was found and finally laid to rest.

On my gravestone, it read: "Sarah May was a loving daughter." Reading that made me cry. I *was* a loving daughter. Why did my Mummy not love me enough to protect me? Now that she was caught I thought I would find my path to peace—but it didn't come. I still remained here.

I followed Mummy to prison. The other inmates there bullied her for being a child killer.

"She was a demon child, I had to put up with her bad attitude for eight years! If she lived with you, you'd have lost it too. I didn't mean for her to die," Mummy said, almost sounding remorseful.

"Do you feel bad for what you did to me, Mummy?"

"Go away, this all your doing," she said.

"What did I do wrong Mummy?" I asked

"If you left me alone I wouldn't be in here being treated like a dog," she said.

"What about what you did to me Mummy? You hurt me."

"You shouldn't have been so rude and it was an accident. You weren't meant to..." she trailed off.

"What? Die? But I did," I said. hoping she would see the errors of her way, but she didn't — she just told me leave her alone.

So once again I sang *Bleeding Love* over and over again. Mummy wasn't able to sleep at all until eventually she couldn't take it. She took an overdose and took her own life.

Now she was the one out of her body. She stared at herself for a long time.

"Strange looking back at yourself," I said to her.

She jumped, scared, away from me. "I thought I got rid of you but you're still here. I took my own life to get away from you!" she screamed at me.

I didn't understand why she hated me so much. She chose to have me and then she hurt me. Others were here now. They had masked faces and red, angry-looking eyes. I was really afraid. As they edged forward, I moved back, but they weren't here for me. They grabbed Mummy by the arms

and dragged her away kicking and screaming.

"I'm sorry! All right, I'm sorry!" she screamed, but it was all a little too late as others took her to a place. I did not want to have anything to do with them. However, true justice had been served.

Now the light shone upon me, and I could feel peace encompass me in the warmth of its embrace.

Truly, revenge was a dish best served cold, after all.

© Lubna Sengul 2016. All rights reserved.

+++

13

CONFESSIONS

Julie M. Brown

"He who seeks vengeance must dig two graves - one for his enemy and one for himself." ~ Chinese Proverb

1974

The priest clung to the side of the small motorboat, his body below the surface of the lake. Water dripped from his nose, wisps of hair plastered to his balding head. His fingers, curled over the boat's edge, were turning blue. "Please Anthony, you don't want to do this."

The young man sitting in the boat shook his head, ignoring the dark clouds and the promise of rain. "You have no idea what I want, Father."

Father O'Neal struggled to lift to his body out of the water. "I have confessed my sins, Anthony. God has forgiven me, and so must you."

Anthony spit at him. The boat listed as the priest again tried to hoist himself up. Anthony tightened his jacket around his body. Watching his teacher suffer gave him no joy.

With great effort, O'Neal raised one leg and hooked his foot over the edge. He bellowed with the strain. Anthony pushed the priest's boot back over the edge. It splashed when it hit the water.

"No!" O'Neal cried.

"I'm sorry, Father," Anthony said. "But this is what we learned from you. An eye for an eye ..."

"I didn't kill Jimmy."

Anthony let out a bitter laugh. "You can't possibly believe that, Father."

O'Neal rested his forehead on the edge of the boat between his hands and took quick, short breaths. Anthony was tempted to uncurl the old man's fingers and let him drop into the lake. O'Neal's coat, now heavy as lead, would drag him down. It would not be a painful death - drowning was supposed to be peaceful. Anthony prayed Jimmy's death had been peaceful. But he doubted it.

"Your brother took his own life, Anthony."

"Because of what you did to him." Anthony looked at the box between his feet, the box that contained Jimmy's ashes. The ashes he would scatter in the lake where the brothers used to play and fish and swim. "He loved you so much." Tears filled Anthony's eyes, and he wiped them away with his sleeve. He still could hear Jimmy's laughter, as if it lived in the wind blowing over the water.

"I know," Father O'Neal said, coughing. "And I pr ... pray for him every day, for you both."

"Don't! Me and Jimmy don't want your prayers. Not anymore!"

The man's eyes, bluer than the lake, opened wide with fear.

"I begged you to leave him alone, Father. Wasn't I enough? I did everything you asked of me, everything!"

"You did. You ... were ... such a g ... good boy." His words came in short bursts. Father O'Neal's hands began to slip, and the water rose over his face until only the top of his head could be seen.

Anthony reached down, grabbed one of O'Neal's arms, and heaved him over the side of the boat. The priest collapsed onto the floorboard in front of the bench where Anthony sat. With his cheek resting in a shallow pool of water, he choked and gasped, then lifted his head to look at Anthony. "Bless you, my son. I forgive you. God forgives you."

Anthony trembled with fury. "I don't seek forgiveness, Father. And I haven't confessed." He threw an old towel at the priest's face. "I'm just not ready for you to die."

In the fading sunlight, the man Anthony had once revered looked broken and terrified. The Priest pushed himself up and sat on the bench across from his former student, shivering and trying to peel off his sodden coat.

Anthony watched him struggle, and a small part of him felt pity. Father O'Neal had been his family's savior.

Anthony's mother, widowed and destitute with two little boys, had gone to the church for help, and Father O'Neal, handsome, steadfast, authoritative, had rescued her. He counseled her through her grief, helped her find comfort in God's loving hands, and took part in rearing her sons, making sure they went to school and church and confession; teaching them to honor their mother, to do their chores, to study hard, and to respect authority. Obedience. One of the most important lessons.

"You meant everything to us," Anthony said. "I trusted you."

Father O'Neal wrapped the towel around his shoulders like a cloak. He placed a hand on Anthony's knee. "My son," he said, his voice calm, as if he were gaining control. "We came to the lake to scatter Jimmy's ashes. That's what you told me you wanted, for us to pray and lay Jimmy to rest together."

Anthony smacked the priest's hand off his leg. "I lied, just like you, Father. You lied to get us to come over, to sit closer, to take off our clothes. You used to say: When you please your priest, you please God ... And I believed every word of it. Did you confess to that? To lying and tricking us into letting you ..." Anthony couldn't say the words, couldn't speak of what he'd allowed his priest to do – the sins he'd committed at Father O'Neal's behest. For years, he tolerated, accepted even, his priest's abuse, too ashamed to tell his mother and terrified of losing Father O'Neal's support and love. He kept the secret, as did Jimmy. A sob caught in Anthony's throat.

Father O'Neal straightened his shoulders, he raised his chin, the same way he did when the boys were his students. It made Anthony feel vulnerable and young. But only for a moment.

"I'm not intimidated by you anymore, Father. And I can throw you back into the lake anytime I want."

O'Neal shrank, like a retreating animal. "What do you want from me, Anthony? What can I do now? Jimmy is gone, and I'm devastated he killed himself, but now there's . . ."

"Jimmy didn't kill himself," Anthony shouted, rage broiling inside of him. "You did it! You tortured him."

Anthony pushed his damp hair out of his face. His voice broke. "By the time he jumped off the bridge, he was already dead, and that was your doing, Father. You said if I did what you wanted, you'd leave my brother alone."

"I did. I'm sorry, Anthony," the priest said, his voice full of remorse. "I'm so sorry. But please, my son, don't sacrifice your own soul in order to destroy mine. Vengeance belongs to the Lord!"

Anthony's anger exploded. "Don't quote your fucking bible to me! I don't care if I go to hell. I welcome it, if only to see you burn amongst all the sinners who will never sit with God!"

"I repented! I have earned my way back! I will have my place in heaven."

Anthony lowered his hands. He saw desperation in O'Neal's eyes. "Then why are you afraid to die?"

The priest's mouth hung open, his eyes lost focus. He blinked, and his face drained of color. It revealed everything. Not all had been confessed. Father O'Neal was scared of dying in a state of mortal sin.

The priest fell to his knees, hands clasped, his lips moving in silent prayer.

"Fool!" Anthony shouted at O'Neal. "Don't waste your prayers. The God I know will not redeem you!"

The priest looked up, his face smeared with tears and snot. "My God will hear my prayers, and he will know I am repentant. I will not be condemned!"

O'Neal's fear gave Anthony pause. Despite the priest's perversion and sins, he was still a man of God, and he yearned for salvation. Anthony's power over his survival meant nothing. It was the man's soul that mattered.

Anthony picked up the box and opened it. Half of Jimmy's ashes had been buried in the cemetery beside their father's grave. Anthony stirred what remained with one finger. It wasn't soft and light like wood ash, more like a gritty sand with bits of bone fragment. He looked up. O'Neal was watching him.

"This is all that's left of him." Anthony reached into his jacket pocket and pulled out the rosary Jimmy had worn as an altar boy. He fingered the beads and the crucifix. It had been a gift from Father O'Neal. "Except for this."

O'Neal's chin trembled, his eyes full of regret.

With the rosary wrapped around his fingers, Anthony cast Jimmy's remains into the water. As the last vestiges of ash settled on the surface, a ray of light broke through the clouds and shimmered on the lake. For the first time since his brother's death, Anthony was at peace. Jimmy was in heaven, and one day they would be together again. He tossed the rosary into the water. It joined the ashes and drifted away with the current.

"My brother was good," Anthony said. "He would have been a great man."

"I know," said the priest, his voice small and raspy.

"I used to tease him because he loved going to church. I mean, what kid wants to go to church?" Anthony eyed Father O'Neal. "Everything was so clear to him. He loved everyone, but most of all he loved God. Did you know that he considered becoming a priest?"

O'Neal pressed his lips together. He shook his head. "I . . . I did not."

"He did, but he gave up. You ruined him." Anthony squeezed his eyes closed and pictured his little brother with

the boyish grin and curly blond hair. "He would have been a good priest, Father, don't you think?"

"I have no doubt."

Anthony looked into Father O'Neal's blue eyes, and he felt nothing. No sadness or regret or compassion for the tormented priest. "Last month, right before Jimmy died, we were drinking beer, a lot of beer, and Jimmy said we should forgive you. For the sake of our own salvation, we must try to forgive."

"Jimmy forgave me?" O'Neal asked, his eyes wide with hope.

"No. Well, I don't know. He said he was trying to. But you stole his innocence, and then you destroyed his faith. How could he forgive that? Because of you, he lost his faith in God."

The mist turned to rain, as if angels were weeping.

They'd been on the lake for hours, and Anthony was tired. He was cold and hungry. He needed to get home, to let his mother know her younger son was in heaven and at peace.

"We're going in," he said to the priest.

O'Neal let out an audible sigh of relief. "You're not going kill me?"

"No."

"And will you forgive me? Will you try?"

Anthony toyed with the box that had held his brother's ashes. "No," he said. "I will never forgive you. I don't even think I can forgive God."

"That breaks my heart, Anthony, truly. No matter what happens, what you do, I pray you are able to find your way back to God."

Anthony took a deep breath. He turned toward the back of the boat and pulled the starter cord. The engine made a grinding noise, but it refused to turn. He tried again, using the choke, but the motor failed to turn over.

"What's wrong?" O'Neal asked.

"Don't know." Anthony lifted the two-stroke outboard motor out of the water and examined it. Something had jammed up the propeller. In the half-light, it was difficult to see anything amid the lake muck and weeds wrapped around three-blade prop. As he pulled away the debris, his fingers felt a linked chain stuck around the propeller and shaft.

Trying to unravel the obstruction, Anthony felt the distinct shape of a crucifix, Jimmy's crucifix. He tried to wriggle it out, but it was jammed in tight and wouldn't budge. He lowered the motor back into the water. Maybe another try would loosen it. He pulled the starter cord, and the cord snapped.

Rain came down in sheets. The small boat rose and fell as the wind churned up waves. Anthony looked toward shore. They were about a half mile out. Anthony eyed O'Neal. How old was he? Sixty, sixty-five? Could he swim the distance?

As if the priest had read Anthony's mind, he said, "I don't think I can swim that far."

Anthony ran a hand through his wet hair. No matter how much he hated O'Neal, how could he abandon him? The boat lifted with a wave and dropped hard on the water. "I won't leave you."

"Of course you will," O'Neal said, his hair blowing like thin, silvery threads.

Anthony didn't understand. "What do you mean?"

"Have you forgotten how close we once were? How well I knew you? You're a survivor, Anthony." A wave splashed over the side of the boat, and Father O'Neal grasped the edge of his bench. "You have an iron will to endure and to be. Just . . . to be."

Anthony considered the priest's words. Anthony had overcome so much, and he survived it all. He lost every man he ever loved - his dad, his priest, his brother. Yet he still wanted to live. "Maybe you're right."

O'Neal shivered. "I guess you'll have your revenge after all."

Anthony removed his shoes and socks. "I don't want revenge, not anymore." He peeled off his jacket. "If I make it to shore, I'll send help. Or you can come with me." Anthony stripped down to his underwear, unashamed. He couldn't help but recognize the irony of undressing in front of the priest one last time. He stood. "The choice is yours, Father. It always was. I don't care what happens, whether you live or die. As you said, vengeance belongs to the Lord." Without looking back, Anthony dove into the lake.

It took at least an hour to swim through the rough water. At times, he doubted he would make it. His chest ached, his muscles cramped, his lungs stung. At the halfway point, he glanced back, but O'Neal and the little boat were nowhere in sight.

He arrived at the dock, and three men dragged him out of the water. He coughed and sputtered.

"Jesus Christ!" one of the men said. "What the hell happened?"

"Boat . . . disabled, 'bout half-mile out." Anthony felt like he might vomit. "Man still out there . . . needs rescue."

He tried to get up, but his arms gave way, and he collapsed onto the wet boards of the rickety pier.

"I'll call the guard," one of the men said, running to the boathouse. The others helped Anthony to his feet. One of them wrapped a jacket around his shoulders and helped him walk to shore.

The Coast Guard searched for three days, but neither the priest nor the boat were found.

A month later, Anthony went to church. He had not been to confession in many years. It was time.

There was someone in the confessional. Anthony waited impatiently, and, for a brief moment, he considered leaving. The little door opened. A woman came out wiping her eyes, a soft smile around her lips. Anthony sensed her relief.

Taking a deep breath, Anthony entered the confessional with his rosary wrapped around his hand, the rosary Father O'Neal had given him. The priest behind the screen cleared his throat.

Anthony made the sign of the cross. "Forgive me, Father, for I have sinned . . ." He started to cry.

"How long since your last confession, my son?"

"I don't know. Years."

"What sins do you wish to confess?" The priest's voice was calm, compassionate.

Anthony did not know where to begin. So many sins committed, from the tiniest misstep to the most heinous act. It had been so long, he'd forgotten the rituals and the words. Emotion overcame him.

"Do not despair, my son. Confess, and redemption will be yours. Now recite your sins, it doesn't matter how

many you wish . . ."

"There's only one, Father." Anthony covered his face with both hands, tears of shame and sadness and, most of all, anger. "I . . . I . . ."

"You what?"

"I hate God! I have no faith anymore, and I need to . . ."

Father O'Neal's words echoed: I pray you are able to find your way back to God.

"I need to find my way back, Father, but how will I ever forgive God?" As soon as he said the words, he dropped to his knees, hands clasped. Just asking the question gave him hope; it opened the door to salvation. The burden Anthony had been carrying since the first time Father O'Neal touched him began to lift.

© JULIE M. BROWN 2016. ALL RIGHTS RESERVED.
+++

14

TERRESTRIAL TRAITOR

Jeremy Croston

Part I:

The Briefing

We never had a chance.

The day our home was invaded by the Centaries, Earth was very much in danger. A human-like race with technology well past our own capabilities, they were here to dominate and rule. However, Earth didn't just roll over and play dead. Seriously out-gunned, we fought back. In fact, there are still pockets of resistance all over the world. My name is Jeremiah Collins, and I'm a Captain in the Fifth Guard, a resistance force based in what used to be Washington, D.C.

And I'm also a traitor to my people.

They got to me after the Fall of London. My wife and two kids were dead. The only thing that kept me going most days was booze, and a lot of it. Then *she* came - a Centari

who could've been a twin for Cassandra, my wife. Her name was Eliah and she was the vision of perfection I needed. She of course had the Centari stripes under her eyes, like a football player's eye black, and was much taller, but still. The moment she came into my life and separated me from the whiskey bottles, I was captivated. If her mission was to find someone so far down in life, that just the chance to *feel* again would get them to betray Earth, she succeeded.

The more and more time we spent together, I knew there was a spark. Sure, she wasn't from Earth and her people were hell bent on wiping us out to take what was ours, but the heart wants what it desires. I did everything she asked of me, no matter the cost. Each successful mission brought us closer together.

To this day I tell myself I had no choice.

I joined the Fifth Guard shortly afterwards; my previous Army experience was a huge boost for them. Quickly, I gained the trust of General Adam Eiger and was soon promoted to 2nd Officer. Another year later and I was named Captain. The job as the Captain is to put together strikes against the Centaries different outposts. It was the perfect place for a mole like me.

Once in the Fifth Guard, Eliah stayed on as my handler. She stayed on as even more than that - we fell in love, completely. Any shreds of loyalty to Earth were completely gone - the former Jeremiah Collins was no longer. I could only imagine what my wife and kids thought of me, but I forced those feelings out. Like I said, a part of me was dead.

"Collins, we've got a report of a Centari outpost that's been abandoned in the outskirts of Richmond."

My head looked up from my computer. I'd been pretending to read the latest news cycling about the Resistance forces. I stood at attention and saluted the General. "That's great news, General Eiger, sir."

The steel-haired man with broad shoulders and a powerful built saluted me back. He respected me so much. "After the success on your last assassination mission, we want you to lead the charge."

My last mission; that was a joke. I had told Eliah that they wanted me to take down a Centari who was responsible for the deaths of two Resistance leaders. In order to keep my good faith up, she took the assignment on for me and brought me his weapon.

General Eiger had been crowing for weeks about that success.

I turned my screen from the news to his bulletin channel. The first thing that popped up was a grainy picture taken at night. Even with the poor quality, you could see the outline of the Centari outpost; the familiar two towers anchored at the two exit points. "Does intel have any idea what's being held there, sir?"

He looked around before answering. "We've been told this outpost was used as a central command for their spy network." Eiger rubbed his hands together greedily. "If we're lucky, we might be able to get all the names of the humans working for them."

My stomach dropped. I couldn't let the General see my immediate fear and discomfort. "I'll gladly take the lead on this mission. If we can root out the traitors, that'll be a big blow to their operation on Earth."

His powerful hand hit my shoulder. "I knew I could

count on you, son. The mission briefing is in two hours and your team will roll out in twelve. Good luck."

+

Sitting in a deserted alley in what used to be the Capital of the United States, I waited for Eliah to show. I only had about an hour and a half before I needed to get back to the resistance base for the briefing. Fortunately, no one came into the city, it was way too dangerous.

I pulled my hood up over my face to keep the dust that whipped around out of my face. The Centaries had used a weapon called an Asteroid Pulsar to bring one down from space and wipe out large cities. The dust was a byproduct of such a calculated strike. If you breathed in too much of it, you were as good as dead.

"Jeremiah, is that you?"

The soft voice brought me out of my thoughts. Turning to the opposite end of the alley, Eliah was there in her soldier uniform. Where mine was bulky, brown, and covered in pockets, the Centari uniform was sleek. Black material hugged her perfect body and as she took off her helmet, white-blond hair cascaded down to her shoulders. She was the visual of perfection.

I returned a muffled answer. "Yeah, it's me my love."

We quickly met each other in the middle and hugged. "You weren't followed?"

"No, I told them I was doing a recon assignment in the city. No one comes in here unless they have to."

A smile broke across her face, showing perfect white teeth. The only difference, hers were sharp at the ends over

the squared bluntness of humans.

We kissed before I broke into the reason of my calling. "The Resistance found a base outside of Richmond that was abandoned."

"Yes, that was once used as a turning facility, for humans who were not as open-minded as you."

She confirmed what the General told me. "Is there any chance my cover will be blown if they capture that outpost?"

She shook her head and rubbed my covered face gently. "Operations have moved, but if you could blow that place up, it'd be a great help to us." With a wink, "I'll make sure you have no other choice."

With my new objective given to me, I kissed her once again before returning to base.

+

There were six of us in the briefing—Eiger and myself, along with weapons experts Jerry Fowler and Josh Green, and scouts Hank Jones and Melissa Pan.

Eiger was leading the briefing, pacing the room as he gathered his thoughts. "This mission carries the highest of security clearances. No one else but the people in this room knows about the task at hand."

The five of us he was talking to each looked around warily. I'd worked with Fowler and Pan before, but not the others.

The General continued, "As I told each of you just hours ago, we've discovered an old outpost now abandoned by the Centaries. Jones, brief the folks on what your scouts found."

Hank Jones was a small man with eagle-like eyes. His brown hair was all but shaved off and his face wore the scars of a great many battles. "My scouts weren't able to penetrate the walls or the defense system that is still active there, but in the outlying areas, we found clues that this may have been the command center for their human spies."

A few gasps came from the room. "Human spies... I thought that was an urban legend." Jerry Fowler seemed shaken up at the idea of this. "You mean the Centaries are using them against us?"

"We don't know, Fowler." Eiger seemed unsure himself, which was probably the main reason for this mission. "All we know is we need to grab whatever information that outpost has before they come back and blow it to Kingdom Come."

Our attention went back to Hank. "There's a service road that leads to the backside of the outpost. From there, we can make an initial breach and get out as quickly as we can."

I raised my hand. "You said defense systems that are still online—what are you referring to?"

"The usual; pulse guns that are mounted on the lookouts and more than likely concussion bombs in the ground." He gestured for Melissa Pan to stand up. "Pan here will be able to lead us safely in, but it'll be slow. Once in the base, we can disable their leftovers."

There was more to be said, but we'd never get the chance as Eiger ended the briefing. "Gentlemen, lady, the time for chatting is over. Securing the compound and taking whatever the Centaries left behind could be the first step is winning our planet back. Trust each other and God speed."

Part 2:

The Outpost

I was lying in bed with the enemy.

To my planet at least, but to me she was my everything. I never thought I'd be happy again, able to feel true emotion. Then she came into my life and brought my back from the ashes. True, it was at the cost of my loyalty to the human race, but where were most of them when I was drowning in sorrow? That's how I justified it to myself anyway.

Her long finger ran over my chest. "There's no need to be nervous, Jeremiah. Nothing that's there can be traced back to you."

That had crossed my mind a bit, but that's not what was bugging me. "How many humans are spies for the Centari Empire?"

"A few hundred tops. We only choose those we believe will be strong once the assimilation is complete."

I've heard her mention the assimilation before, when the Resistance is wiped out and the resources on Earth are mined and taken back to their home world. So she had plans to take me back with her, to whatever barren wasteland of a planet they'd come from.

I was also getting more and more curious about my handler. She seemed to have knowledge that would be over the level of a foot soldier. Eliah knew things that seemed like only top officials would know and always made

assurances I was very surprised she was able to keep. Just who was she and was I myself in danger? I wasn't sure how to ask these questions without rocking the boat. So for the time being, I stayed quiet.

The alarm on my Resistance-issued watch went off, it was time to begin. "Is everything squared away at your end?"

She leaned over and wrapped me up tight. I knew she wanted more time here, that her needs were never quite sated. "Yes, my love. You will have ample opportunity and reason to make sure that place ends up in flames."

Reluctantly, I rolled out of bed. "I won't fail."

That much was true. I never had.

+

When I arrived at the base, the night was still dominating the sky. Under the cover of darkness, as it was a new moon, only the six of us from the briefing were there. Eiger was ready to hand out his final proclamations. "Troops, we don't know what will happen. Get there safe, watch each other's backs, and do what must be done."

We all moved to attention and saluted him.

"Last, but not least—I trust each of you with my life. Find out what you can so we can eliminate those who willingly betrayed our planet. For those traitors, only a swift death awaits them."

Under my mask, I may have showed a sign of regret for my actions, but no one else would ever see it. With one final salute, the five of us assigned to infiltrate the outpost gathered into our armored vehicle and pulled out of the base.

There was no turning back now—we were on our way to Richmond.

I was behind the wheel and Hank Jones was the co-pilot. We didn't have much to say, just the occasional question and answer about the directions. We were using back roads, as the Centaries had destroyed most of the main highways as a way to cripple us and keep us segmented.

The morning sun was beginning to break the horizon when Jones had me pull off to the side of the road. I drove down aways into a ditch and stopped. He called to those in the back. "This is it. Time to move out."

Before we left, I commanded us to cover our vehicle with debris, sticks, leaves, whatever, so no one would see us out here. It was a sound strategy, even though I knew it wouldn't make much of a difference. They knew we were going to be coming.

We hiked through the forest to the service road Hank had told us about. Off in the distance, the Centari outpost was an eyesore. Maybe a mile away, the tower that served as the back entrance stood there like a black sentinel, daring us to challenge it and the defenses that would be posted. Pulse guns would be littered all over the side of the building, that I knew.

Melissa jumped to the front of the line. "Follow me step for step. I can see the telltale signs of a concussion bomb, but chances are, we'll have a small window to maneuver with."

We did as the young scout ordered us to. In a life or death situation, you willingly took orders from someone with greater knowledge than you, no matter age or sex. Pan was going to get us to our objective, and she was going to do

it safely. Inching forward, we fell in line behind her and, at least for me, holding my breath the entire time.

As we crept closer, the pulse guns came into view. Pan held up a fist, indicating we needed to stop. No one said a word as she and Jones appraised the situation. Tense silence followed in those moments, unsure if we needed to take evasive action and, in doing so, risk setting off a concussion bomb. Then, "The pulse guns seem to be offline. We keep going as planned."

With Jones giving the all clear, I had to wonder if this wasn't the work of Eliah. Most outposts, even ones that were sparsely manned or completely shut down, had their systems operational. Even Jones said in the briefing everything was still active. No one else voiced any suspicions, just seemed grateful that one less obstacle needed to be tackled.

When we passed the last of the concussion bombs, the group took a moment to regroup. As the commander I said, "Okay, we all know what to do. Let's keep this quick, the air doesn't feel right."

They nodded at me and grabbed their weapons. Each Resistance soldier was given a rail gun—a modified design from the Centaries pulse guns. The recoil was less, allowing us to handle the weapon, but with the added element of mercury to the blasts, which was deadly to our foes. The problem was the Centaries field uniforms held up very well. Getting a clean blast at one of them for the mercury to do its job was damn near impossible.

The door to the outpost was closed, but as I closed in on it, the digital lock used was broken. "I think we're walking into a trap."

"What makes you say that, Captain?"

"How many raids have you ever seen the lock disabled, Fowler?"

At my point, he conceded. "What do we do from here?"

I was about to say blow the place to bits, but the door shot forward, sending us scrambling. Two Centaries charged out and began raining fire down upon us. We had no choice but to retreat into the woods just off to the side for cover. Fowler, Green, and I returned fire as Pan attended to a wounded Jones. It looked as if he took a blast to the knee. It was a mess.

No others came out beside the two warriors engaged with us. We were in a dogfight and the odds weren't in our favor. Looking down, "Jones, do you have a rabbit grenade on you?"

He winced in pain but answered. "Yeah, in my right leg pocket." Pan understood and dug it out.

I caught it, with Green and Fowler still letting loose the rail blasts. A rabbit grenade was a nasty little invention that was full of solidified mercury pellets. They were tricky to make and the amount of mercury it took to make them made these things a luxury, but this situation called for it. Unhooking the pin, I lobbed the rabbit towards the Centaries. At impact, they screamed in horror and pain as the mercury pellets ripped into their bodies.

They were dead in seconds.

Even with our enemy dead, we still had major issues. Jones was in no shape to continue, meaning we were about to split up. Lesser numbers were never a good thing. "Pan, take Fowler with you and get Jones back to the transport." I looked to Green. "It'll just be the two of us."

No one liked this situation, but as Captain, it was my prerogative to issue the orders. Pan would be needed to navigate the bomb field and Fowler would provide cover now that our presence was known. Before they left, I had one last order. "Pan, once they make it back safely, I need you to get down here one last time. Green and I will need an escort back."

She saluted me. "Sir, yes, sir."

With that, we departed towards the base while they struggled to get Jones up and mobile.

+

The air inside was muggy, a stark contrast to the cold wind whipping around the outside of the outpost. I knew their home planet was quite a bit hotter than Earth, but never before had a base felt as swamp-like as this. We entered the first control room, just off to the side of the entrance door, there was nothing.

"Captain, this place looks long abandoned. Why would they have sentries posted here?"

Again, I was thankful that my face was fully covered. "This is war, Green. If they think we can use this station, they'll make sure to give it a small amount of defense."

He pressed the issue. "Then the pulse guns on the tower should've been activated. Something's not adding up. We both know it."

I didn't know what he knew or was even assuming. This conversation put me even further on edge. "You think someone tipped them off?"

He was beside me now. "Yeah I do. Ever since Eiger

told us about human spies, I couldn't help but think we have a traitor in our own ranks."

"That's a strong statement to make."

As soon as Eiger dropped even the subtlest of doubt, I knew something like this would happen. You can't tell people about human spies without them seeing them at every corner. Granted, Green was more right than he could ever guess, but I was hopeful this was just paranoia speaking and not something concrete.

I pressed him. "What are you thinking? Spit it out before we go any further."

He looked hesitant. Then, "Jones, sir." He took a deep sigh. "I mean, he's our scout and he brought us here. Doesn't it make sense, especially since he conveniently got shot in a non-fatal place? Here we are risking our necks for something that's probably not here."

It would've been ironic if Jones was a spy, but Eliah already told me I was the only one under her command in this unit. I shouldn't have been so trusting, but the bond we had was great. "I admire your vigilance, I really do." Still, I needed this place to go up in flames. "We at least have to attempt this, if only to prove your thoughts are correct."

We walked back into the corridor and I pointed to a door at the far end of the hallway. Green and I had our guns ready. When we reached our destination, I quickly grabbed the door handle and pushed it forward. All we could see is dark.

Then it happened.

Quicker than a human could move, a shape whisked out of the shadows and impaled Green with a long, red blade.

He fell to the ground, no longer with me, never realizing what happened.

My eyes went back to the weapon that took his life. I'd only seen those once before. They were the weapons of the Centari royal family. Where the average Centari carried a gun and a small knife, the royal family carried a blade fit of their honor. If one was here...

The attacker pulled *her* hood down.

"Eliah?"

Wiping the blood from the now deceased Green off her sword before sheathing it, my handler, my lover smiled at me. "Jeremiah, we have just a minute before—"

"Eliah, are you a member of the royal family?"

My question stopped whatever she was going to say. For the first time, she looked uncomfortable with a question I asked her. "Yes. I was hoping you wouldn't have noticed the shade of my sword."

I didn't know how to feel. "What does this mean?"

Behind me, I heard a beeping tone. It was steady at first but gradually picked up in tempo. "Jeremiah, we must—"

"Not before you answer my question. Please Eliah, I am owed that much."

As the beeping increased, "I am. My people call me Queen Eliah the XII." My jaw dropped. "I am the leader of my people, the strongest of the Centari."

Part 3:

The Choice

There was just one last act to play.

When we reached the base, the group still hadn't been able to put together what happened. I hadn't lied to them either; it was a trap set by the Queen of the Centari herself. She wanted to see what kind of resistance the humans were capable of. In the end, we'd been the test subjects and it had cost Green his life.

I parked the vehicle in the base hanger. There was one last thing they didn't need to know—a homing beacon had been placed on this transport. Eliah decided it was time to wipe out such a well-organized group such as the Fifth Guard. In her eyes, we were becoming a genuine threat that needed to be extinguished now.

We had made it out of the back of the outpost opposite where my team entered before the bomb went off. She placed the beacon in my hand and promised me a place by her side when this was all over. She chose me because much like me, she had felt the pain of losing a spouse and our shared pain created a bond stronger than she could've imagined.

With that heartfelt confession, I gave in to my heart, my lust and completed my full betrayal of my people.

"I'll report to Eiger what happened." No one looked as if they wanted to take that job. "Take some time and let what happened at that outpost reinforce your belief in the cause."

As I walked into the base, people saw my facial expression. It was known what to look for when a mission went south. They may not have known the details, but they had to know we'd just come back from something. There was just silence as I passed and entered Eiger's office.

I closed the door. "It was a trap."

He looked up from his papers. "How bad?"

"We lost Green and Jones is hurt bad. That's not the problem, General." I leaned down close. "The trap was executed by the Queen of the Centari. She was testing our strength."

Eiger's face went white, the kind that tells you nothing good is about to happen. "There had been rumors the royal family was in play, but thank you for unwittingly confirming that for us, you fool. Only you would've been able to identify Eliah without hesitation..." He got up from his desk. "Now we are left in a precarious spot."

"What do you mean?"

He reached into his jacket. When he turned around, he had an old style revolver pointed at me. "It means your usefulness to the cause is up."

I had no idea what was going on. "General, what are you talking about?"

He laughed, very joyfully at my surprise it seemed. "Come now, Jeremiah, I know all about your liaison with the Queen. My employers made sure I knew of your every move the moment you stepped on this base."

Was this a betrayal inside a betrayal? "You work for the Centaries too?"

He couldn't answer before the first blast rocked the base. Eliah was here with her forces. Eiger had stumbled a

bit and dropped his gun. It was too far from where I was to grab it, so I tried to run out of the office. Before I made it, the door flew open and slammed me back to the ground. A large Centari was blocking the path. "Leaving so soon, Mister Collins?"

The large figure towered over me.

"I don't understand?"

Eiger joined the Centari lording over me. "Captain Collins, I would like to introduce you to the one who will take this even farther than your beloved Queen. Meet General Ungerthrash."

The name was ridiculous but still somehow suited the powerful Centari. "Eiger, is everything ready for Eliah's arrival?"

The other traitor in the room saluted him just as we had recognized Eiger's rank before. "It is. Once her forces are in a centralized location, we can set off the nuclear weapon just underneath."

There was a nuke under the base? "Eiger, are you insane?"

"No, Jeremiah, like you I'm not. I just happened to pick the winning side."

Instead of killing me there, the two of them left me on the floor and bolted me in, from the outside.

+

There was too much happening to even process what twist just occurred. I was locked in Eiger's room as the fighting from the Centari and the human resistance picked up. Neither side knew about the nuke Eiger apparently armed

under the base and there was little time to warn anyone.

Looking around the room, I saw my escape chance—an old air duct.

The rusted bolts came out easily enough and it was just the right size for me to squeeze into. It took work, but I churned my body forward, getting into the next duct and finally out a ventilation shaft two rooms over.

The Centari forces must've already been here. Five humans were dead, including Melissa Pan. My heart ached for a second, but then I knew that was going to happen. Pushing her face from my eyes, I ran from the room and out into the mess.

Centaries were engaged at all points in the base. I grabbed a rail gun from one of the corpses in the room and pushed down my field garb. I wasn't going to actively engage any targets, but I'd be a fool not to arm myself. Thankfully, with all the major skirmishes happening, no one gave much attention to a random solider running with no pattern or reason.

I broke out of the main part of the base into the hangar. It was there I saw two Centaries engaged in a duel—one with a red sword of the royal family and the other with a standard issue black sword. It was the Queen and the General, with Eiger off to the side. Lining up my shot, I took my former general down with one right to the chest. Ungerthrash didn't even acknowledge his death.

There was one last conundrum for me to solve. I had to assume Eiger loaded the nuke at some point after locking me in the room. What would I do? Save Eliah or the humans who I had served with? The decision was easy. I lined my rail gun up and sent a direct hit through his visor.

The blast entered his eye and exited out the back of his head. The body of the Ungerthrash collapsed to the ground.

Eliah looked up to see where the attack came from. I removed my coverings. "Do you have a transport?" I hoped the urgency of my voice told me to act quickly.

"Outside, my jump ship is docked, why?"

"Eiger and Ungerthrash loaded a nuke; we need to get out of here now!"

I leapt down and began running out the hangar bay door. Eliah followed me quickly and we didn't stop until we reached her jump ship. She quickly got into the pilot's seat and fired up the engines. I locked myself in, preparing for the take off. The engines roared to life just in time and we blasted off, away from the base. As we hurtled through the air, a large mushroom cloud appeared behind us, killing thousands of humans and Centaries alike.

+

The war on Earth ended shortly thereafter. With the fall of the Fifth Guard, many others began to either outright surrender or escape into the great unknown, away from everything. It took the Centaries less than a year to strip the Earth of its minerals and begin their preparations to return to their own planet.

General Ungerthrash's own betrayal of the royal family didn't go unnoticed either. Dissenters were routed out by Eliah and put to death, very publicly. The iron fist of the royal family once again held on to the reigns of the empire.

What happened to me? That's a fair question. I stayed in the shadows after the nuclear disaster at Washington,

D.C. I continued to be faithful to Eliah alone, but the events shook me to my core. I chose my heart over my race and I allowed a great many people to die. That was on me.

After the war was over, I was declared the Queen's Consort and all the privileges that went along with that, including total access to all their ships and equipment. As soon as they were done with the Earth, the fleet began to move out.

They left without me though. I could only begin to imagine the look on Eliah's face when she realized I wasn't on her flagship. It was probably around the same time all the explosions went off, high in space, destroying their fleet. I watched, alone, from a desolate spot of land as the ships went up in fiery chaos.

It had taken years of covert movements and subterfuge. I'd never recover from the depths I had to plumb to make what happened a reality. However, the moment Eliah came into my life, I formed a plan—earn the trust of the Centari and, from the shadows, become their Angel of Death. At the moment of their greatest victory, deliver their ultimate defeat. Earth's revenge was complete.

My name is Jeremiah Collins and I am not a traitor.

© JEREMY CROSTON 2016. ALL RIGHTS RESERVED.
+++

15

RED QUEEN CHECK

Elizabeth Horton-Newton

The red gown clung to her body like a second skin. It was apparent to everyone she wore no undergarments. Her short platinum blond hair stood out in strong contrast to her tanned skin. The head of every man in the room turned as she passed. Every woman's head turned as well, some envious, some desirous. Mark turned as she approached and a smile lit his face. He loved it when she came into a room looking like this. All eyes were on her and she was his, all his.

He slipped an arm around her waist, his hand grazing her naked lower back where the silken fabric of her dress ended. With his other hand he gave her a glass of champagne. The bubbles tickled her nose as she lifted the crystal to her moist pink lips and sipped delicately. "Um. That's nice."

Moving his mouth next to her ear he murmured, "It should be nice. It's the best they have." Noting the small lines that had begun to appear around her eyes he frowned

slightly. Studying her face closely he saw no additional signs of aging and nodded imperceptibly.

Her eyes blinked slowly, the long, full lashes complementing the sky blue of the irises. "I wouldn't expect any less."

Turning back to the two gentlemen who stood nearby, Mark introduced her. "My girlfriend, Vayda."

Their arms bumped as each man attempted to shake her delicate, long fingered hand. A sultry, throaty chuckle escaped her full, pouting lips. She was well aware of the effect she had on men and women. She allowed each man to touch her fingertips, gracing them with a flash of her perfect white teeth.

As Mark continued to converse with the two men Vayda gazed around the room, sizing up the other guests. Quite a few caught her eye and nodded, indicating their awareness of her presence. Finally, Mark brought his lips close to her ear again, the sultry scent of her perfume that smelled of summer filling his head. "Let's blow this popcorn stand."

Offering him a dazzling smile she allowed her lips to graze his cheek as she whispered, "I definitely feel like blowing something."

Mark felt a swelling in his groin as he waited for the valet to bring his car around. Running his hand up and down Vayda's back he leaned closer allowing the rich musky scent of her to tickle his nose. He held the car door as she slid into the passenger seat, the high slit in her dress opening to reveal a long shapely leg. He noted the valet's eyes travel up that leg and thrilled at the expression of envy that crossed his face.

Once behind the wheel he put the car in drive and guided it out of the parking area. As they rode along the dark and winding road to his ocean view home he laid one hand high on her leg. She spread her thighs slightly, encouraging him to slip his hand between them. He accepted the invitation and delighted at the heat coming from the moistness of her silky panties.

Mark didn't bother to pull into the garage. Leaving the car in the driveway he hurried around to pull Vayda from the front seat and into his arms. They kissed passionately, his hands roaming over her body, eager to feel every inch of her.

"Let's go inside." Her voice was honey, sweet and luxurious in his ears.

Taking her hand, he led her to the front door and inside the darkened front hall. As he turned off the alarm she moved away, heading for the bar in the living room.

"Where are you going?" His voice cracked slightly, his eagerness throbbing against the front of his tailored tuxedo pants.

She tossed her head, then, gave him a sultry smile over her shoulder. "I'm going to make us a couple of drinks."

Following her, he slipped his arms around her waist pulling her back against his obviously aroused front. Nuzzling her ear, he said, "Let's go upstairs."

Vayda wiggled her tight bottom against him. "Go on upstairs and slip into something less restrictive and I'll bring us drinks." Then she bumped her backside against him a little more insistently. "Go on."

Sighing resignedly, he headed for the stairs, pulling off his bowtie as he went.

Moving behind the bar, Vayda poured two tumblers of single malt Scotch and added ice to one. Sliding her hand beneath her dress and into her panties she stretched her long fingers inside her vagina and pulled out a tiny vial. Glancing quickly toward the stairs to be certain Mark was not going to reappear, she emptied the contents of the vial into the beverage that didn't contain ice. Stirring it with her finger until it was blended she then carried both glasses up the stairs.

The sound of Mark emptying his bladder reached her ears and for a moment she grimaced, her lips twisting into an unattractive snarl. She quickly regained herself and set his glass on the night table at his side of the bed.

Mark came into the bedroom, naked and semi erect. He reached for her as she darted past him toward the bathroom, her drink in her hand.

"Hey!" He lost his balance and grabbed the side of the dresser to prevent himself from falling.

Vayda giggled. "I need to pee and wash off. I left your drink. Give me a few minutes. I promise it will be worth it."

Slightly annoyed at having to wait, Mark grumbled and went to his side of the bed. His took a long swallow of his drink as he sat down heavily. The sound of running water and Vayda humming drifted into the bedroom. *"She could be such a tease."* He took another swallow of the Scotch, enjoying the burn as it ran down his throat. But he knew she was right, the wait would be worth it. Her body was glorious, young and firm. He chuckled as he looked down at his own body, middle aged and running to fat in spite of his regular exercise. Still, it didn't matter. He had enough money to get any woman he desired.

Sprawling across the bed some of his drink splashed onto the satin bedspread. "Shit," he swore softly. Sitting up he quickly downed the remainder of his drink and set the glass on the night table. As he was pulling the cover from the bed Vayda returned to the room.

Her body glowed in the low lighting of the room, the bright red of her silk panties contrasting with the shimmery gold of her skin. In a moment she was pushing him back onto the bed, climbing over him, and trailing kisses down the front of his body. The heady and familiar scent of the expensive perfume he supplied her aroused him further, increasing his lust. It was the brand he always bought for his women, the fragrance teasing at the corners of his memory, drawing him back to that very first girl. He had not been attractive in high school and he was far from wealthy in those days. He'd gotten a job cleaning pools for the home owners in the better neighborhoods. There was something delicious about watching the lithe bodies of young, rich girls as they lay in the sun, bodies glistening with oil that smelled of coconut. One hot afternoon he observed them drinking the booze their parents kept out in the bar, unlocked and available but still forbidden.

The combination of heat and alcohol was a prescription for danger. The youngest of the girls, no more than fifteen, her skin smooth as a polished gem stumbled around the pool before tumbling in. He dove in after her and pulled her to safety. They begged him to take her home before their parents returned and found out they had been drinking. They begged, offering anything he wanted, to help them. He recalled the way he hardened, actually aching at the possibility he could have every one of them if he chose.

They helped him lift the petite semi-conscious girl into the front seat of his truck. She was only fifteen but had the body of a woman. As he drove he watched her out of the corner of his eye. If it hadn't been for the seat belt she would have fallen over. As it was her firm young breasts strained against the skimpy swim suit top. Eyes half closed she groaned.

He'd asked if she was going to be sick and when she didn't respond he pulled off the road and down a trail that led to the river. The feel of her skin, slick and hot, beneath his hand aroused him further. Ever so gently he loosened the tie of her top and the strings fell. Watching her face closely for any reaction he slipped one of her breasts free and stared at her hard, pink nipple. Even as he undressed her she didn't react. It was only when he moved on top of her and forced himself inside her that she began to resist. Her struggles were feeble, her hands flailing as she tried to push him away. By the time he got to her driveway she had managed to put her swim suit back on. Her tan no longer glowed golden but was pale and pasty, shocked by what had happened. As she reached to open the truck door he'd grabbed her arm. He'd warned her if she said anything he would tell everyone she asked for it; he'd ruin her reputation. Reminding her he had friends and he knew where she lived he added fear for her to life to fear of humiliation.

For weeks he would jump when someone knocked at the door, certain she had overcome her panic and revealed what he had done. She never said a word to anyone. He never even knew her name. But he knew that scent; the sweet scent of coconut and vanilla, and the odor of her pussy on

his fingers. He didn't wash his hands that night. Instead he laughed to himself when he ate dinner with his parents, taking biscuits from the bowl, using the knife to spread butter, picking fries from his plate and smelling her as he bit into the hot crunchy potato. And that night in his bed as he remembered how she had thrashed beneath him he'd held his fingers beneath his nose as his other hand relived the intense experience.

Groaning loudly, he turned himself over to Vayda's attentions. Fueled both by her ministrations as well as his memories his passion grew so intense he felt lightheaded, almost dizzy with desire. Yet his limbs felt oddly heavy and when he tried to tangle his fingers in her hair in order to push her hot mouth where he most wanted it, his arms flopped uncontrollably.

Then she was on him and her heat enveloped him. She was grinning down at him, her eyes like strange blue lights piercing his brain. The room grew blurry and her face seemed to grow larger until it filled his vision, blocking out everything else.

"What the hell is happening?" he wanted to ask, but his mouth and tongue would not move.

She read the question in his eyes and grinned. "Theda DesJardin." The name rolled off her tongue smoothly. Although his expression did not change she knew instinctively what an impact the name made on him.

He heard the name and a dozen thoughts and images filled his head. Theda. The first time he saw her, sixteen years old in a tiny string bikini on the beach. Theda, barely five feet tall, her hair a dark halo around her deeply tanned face, those piercing blue eyes filled with terror the first time

he took her after weeks of controlling his rapidly growing rapacious hunger. Those piercing blue eyes that he realized looked identical to the eyes now staring down at him.

"She was my cousin; she was like a baby sister to me. We were closer than sisters actually. I knew you were pursuing her. I warned her you were dangerous. But she loved the attention, the gifts, the parties. She believed you would help her with a career as a singer. She had a voice like an angel. She was an angel. You chose to still that voice with your disgusting desires. I knew your money and your dishonest connections would rally to protect you. I knew to attack you with facts would prove fruitless. I also knew your weakness. So I became your weakness."

Mark felt a sharp pain in his left arm radiating into his chest and his breathing, which had become difficult, became more labored.

Vayda leaned to the side and pulled a long thin knife from beneath the mattress.

"Oh God," Mark thought in terror, "She's going to kill me."

Instead she drew the blade along the inner part of her arm and blood began to run down across his chest and onto the bedclothes, the crimson spreading slowly.

He wondered if she was going to murder him and then commit suicide. Taking the knife, she closed the fingers of his left hand around the handle. Dropping the knife onto the bed she proceeded to scratch frantically at his chest and face leaving long red stripes across his flesh. The sharp pain in his chest spread down his arm and he felt as though a fist was lodged beneath his breast bone.

Vayda hopped off the bed and raising her arm above

her head she spun in a circle, first to the left, then to the right. Blood flew from the gash on her arm casting a spray of bright red beads around the room as though a ruby necklace had broken into pieces, stones like flying projectiles.

Mark watched the display unable to flinch when slightly salty, metallic drops landed on his parted lips and insinuated themselves into his open mouth.

Breathing heavily now, Vayda stopped spinning and ripped her panties from her body, tossing them to one side. Her full lips curled into a smile that didn't reach her eyes.

"I could have killed you. But then you would be dead and you would not suffer. Theda suffered. She suffered your vicious attacks. Did you know the medical examiner told us she had not only been raped in every way possible, she had also been penetrated by large objects?" Pointing at his limp phallus she laughed. "It certainly wasn't that pitiful thing, which couldn't give pleasure to a flea. Is that why you chose instruments?"

Vayda's voice seemed to be coming from a distance and her form was surrounded by a wavering outline. "I'm dying," Mark thought. All sound was gone then. All sight no more than a memory.

When Mark's eyes fluttered open he had no idea how much time had passed. Struggling to a sitting position he looked around for Vayda. She was gone. All that remained was the carnage she'd created; broken lamps, overturned chairs, streaks of drying and dried blood. He swung his shaking legs out of the bed and stumbled to the bathroom. Catching sight of himself in the mirror he felt fury building. She had clawed him, leaving shocking red streaks

across his chest and face. He touched them lightly, his fingertips tentatively exploring the wounds. "Bitch!" he thought furiously. "I'll find her and beat her to a pulp. When I'm finished with her, no man will look at her with anything but disgust."

As he reached toward the medicine chest to find some ointment he heard a crashing sound from downstairs. Eyes narrowed, he rushed from the bathroom to catch her destroying his home, his beautiful home. "I'm coming!" He roared as he burst from the bedroom.

Mark stopped short at the top of the stairs seeing several policemen, guns drawn, climbing toward him. They were already aiming for him, the shouted announcement of his arrival warning them. "Hands above your head and turn around slowly," one of the men instructed.

"You don't understand," Mark began. The chest pain caught him once again and all the air seemed to leave his body is a whoosh. He reached up with his right hand to rub his left arm. A look of curiosity lit his bulging eyes.

"Sir! Place your hands on your head and turn around slowly." The man commanded more sternly. The cop had seen that bulgy eyed stare before. It usually signified a cornered criminal was getting ready to do something stupid.

As Mark opened his mouth to protest again he was hit with fifty thousand volts of electricity. His body spasmed as he fell to the floor close to the top step. Suddenly he was sliding and jerking his way down toward the policemen quickly moving backwards. The entire scene was almost comical as the naked man danced down the stairs obscenely and the battle-garbed police fell over one another in an effort to avoid contact with him. Reaching the bottom of

the stairs two of the policemen at the rear of the descending mass tripped over one another and fell awkwardly, one atop the other. One man leaped over the railing and landed indelicately on the highly polished floor, sliding several feet on his ass before flipping over and coming to a hard stop against the wall. The other two officers managed to scatter away from the tangle at the foot of the stairs, leaving room for Mark to come to a full and deadly halt, his head twisted at a peculiar angle, one leg bent crookedly, a bone protruding boldly through stretched skin. He had stopped his gruesome boogie and now lay still, staring blankly through the railing at the cop who was struggling to remove his helmet and swearing loudly.

One of the men who had avoided the jumble of bodies pulled off his helmet shouting, "Shit, shit, shit!" at the top of his lungs. Whether this was an expression of anger or a comment on the stream of feces and urine that trailed down the stairs behind Mark is still in question. Whatever he meant by the exclamations, the fact was Mark was definitely deceased.

Within thirty minutes the house was flooded with crime scene investigators searching for evidence of the crime that had been reported hours earlier. Evidence of the bloody struggle in Mark's bedroom seemed to give confirmation to the account of the murder of Mark's vivacious girlfriend Vayda. While there was no body, there was more than enough blood and debris to confirm something deadly had occurred in the shambles of the bedroom. Bullet holes were discovered in the wall behind the bed, a large and bloody machete type weapon was found in the bathroom. The bathtub appeared to have been recently cleaned and there

was a strong odor of bleach in the air. In spite of the scrubbing, blood spatter remained on the exterior of the tub as well as the base of the toilet and on the dark tiles.

No information would be forthcoming from the presumed-to-be-innocent suspect. However, his threatening response to the police virtually confirmed what the police emergency operator had been told. Someone had heard screams in the still night along with breaking glass and what sounded like gunshots. A while later a car was heard speeding down the road that led away from Mark's home. The caller speculated either the house was being robbed or someone was being killed.

A car had been dispatched and the two officers found Mark's Mercedes parked haphazardly in front of the house, ablaze with lights. Knocking on the door they received no response and called for back-up.

As the sky began to lighten, casting thin streaks of pink and melon above the dark ocean, neighbors gathered on their lawns, murmuring questions and speculating answers.

Reporters with cameras and television trucks were stopped at the foot of Mark's driveway. Some stood, microphones in hand, as they related what little they knew of the events that had occurred in the home of the well-known millionaire. While far from being the wealthiest man in the world, he was rich enough to make the news worthy of an early morning bulletin.

Mark's funeral was a spectacle. His long-ignored daughter Gennifer didn't know any of the people who attended, other than his lawyer. Within four hours of Mark's death Sweetner, MacMillian, and Jones, represented

by old man Sweetner himself, was on the phone. She acted appropriately shocked. In some ways she was shocked. She had no remorse and no regrets; in fact, she experienced a sensation of relief. He'd abandoned her and her mother years before, but not before he'd introduced his then ten-year-old daughter to his depraved world of sexual deviance. When threats of financial ruin were presented to her mother the woman had signed a statement agreeing she would not reveal what she had seen one hot summer day when she'd returned from a trip to the spa. Money managed to dull the memory of her daughter's frightened and stricken expression and the image of her husband rising from between the child's legs. He hadn't even attended her mother's funeral, instead leaving his eighteen-year-old daughter to deal with the arrangements.

Lenore, no longer Vayda but returned to her true identity, also attended the funeral, standing well back in the crowd of mourners. Her hair was now its natural blue-black topped by a small black hat with a veil that discreetly covered much of her face. Without the stiletto heels she always wore when socializing with Mark she was six inches shorter. The breast implants had been removed along with the layers of makeup and she appeared much smaller and younger. She was lost in the crowd just the way she wanted. Her eyes scrutinized the throng from downcast eyes.

Gennifer's eyes also passed over the crowd; men accompanied by beautiful young women. How many of these wealthy men were as immoral as the man who lay in the ornate casket covered with blossoms? She had no idea there was a woman in that mass of mourners who could easily have answered that question.

The heady scent of the assortment of flowers was making Gennifer nauseous. Several times she felt lightheaded. If anyone had noticed she would have explained she was overcome with sadness. Scanning the crowd her stomach tightened.

The media covered the funeral not only because of Mark's wealth and reputation as a great negotiator but because of the scandal surrounding his death. Although lawyers had attempted to conceal the horrors found in his home, copies of letters, photographs of very young girls, DVDs of bondage and S & M, and pictures of the crime scene were leaked to every type of media. While the case of his missing girlfriend, Vayda, remained unsolved most people suspected he had done away with her. Perhaps she'd discovered his stash of pornography and his taste for very young girls. In his mid-forties he still lusted after girls as young as fourteen. News reporters speculated she had threatened to expose him.

In the end, Gennifer used a large portion of his money to set up a residence for women who were escaping abusive husbands; men who had sexually abused their children and beaten their wives. Lenore was lying on the beach when she read about the girl's generosity in the paper. It pleased her to know Gennifer had done so. She expected the girl would have done something similar.

After all, Lenore had seen the Polaroid photos of the girl child who stared into the camera lens, eyes filled with fear and pain. Setting the newspaper down by her chair she leaned back and closed her eyes.

The air was filled with the sounds of children playing in the surf and the laughter of a group of girls who

sunbathed nearby. "Rest in peace my Theda." She did not see the gull that rose high in the sky, dipping its wings in gratitude before flying out over the waves and celebrating its freedom.

© ELIZABETH HORTON-NEWTON 2016. ALL RIGHTS RESERVED.

+++

ABOUT THE AUTHORS

JOSEPH MARK BREWER *[Nothing But The Truth]* grew up near Cincinnati, Ohio, and after many years dividing his time between Japan, Canada, and the United States, settled in Austin, Texas. He is a US Navy veteran and graduated from the University of Kansas with a degree in journalism before beginning a career in the news business. These days, both fiction and non-fiction work demand most of his time. On any given day, it's a toss-up which one prevails. In addition to writing short stories, Joe is the author of the *Shig Sato Mystery Series*. Book 3, *Traitors & Lies*, is now available. Also, please Tweet Joe **@JoeBrewer1**

JULIE M. BROWN *[Confessions]* lives on the Palos Verdes Peninsula, a rural suburb of Los Angeles, with her husband, two sons (who return from school periodically for laundry service and home-made chicken soup) and a pack of mischievous, lovable boxers. She started her career when her boys were little writing freelance . . . news articles, humorous essays, travel escapades, and adventures in motherhood. Her work has appeared in the Daily Breeze, Los Angeles Times, Los Angeles Jewish Journal, and Parenting Magazine. Her first novel, *The Long Dance Home*, was published in 2013 by Mischievous Muse Press, a subsidiary of World Nouveau Publishing. Currently working on her next novel, Julie usually can be found with her laptop and coffee in one of the quiet corners of her local library. Learn more about Julie at **www.juliemayersonbrown.com**.

PAMELA CRANE *[The Scream of Silence]* is a professional juggler. Not the type of juggler who can toss flaming torches in the air, but a juggler of four kids, a writing addiction, a horse rescuer, and a book editor by trade. She lives on the edge (ask her Arabian horse about that—he'll tell you all about their wild adventures while trying to train him!) and she writes on the edge. Her characters and plots are her escape from the real world of dirty diapers and cleaning horse stalls, and she thrives off of an entertaining tale. Pamela is the author of the best-selling psychological thriller *The Admirer's Secret*, Amazon top 20 short story *A Fatal Affair*, and her latest releases *A Secondhand Life* and *A Secondhand Lie*. To pick up a copy of a FREE book, or to find out more about her chaotic existence, visit her website at **www.pamelacrane.com**.

JEREMY CROSTON *[Terrestrial Traitor]* started writing back in the early 2000's when he was at the University of Central Florida to help curb the boredom of the many marketing classes taken. After graduation, the story line for the Ragnarok on Ice series was put in a box never to see the light of day again...or so we thought. His wife found the stories while moving and encouraged him to put it into print. So here we are with the Ragnarok on Ice series available on Amazon and other fine places. Jeremy is married to his wonderful wife and editor Stephanie. In addition to writing, he works in business development for a Fortune 500 company. He enjoys playing soccer, catching up on all things related to Teenage Mutant Ninja Turtles, and watching his dog run around aimlessly.

KEITH DIXON *[Set for Saturday]* was born in Yorkshire and grew up in the Midlands. He's been writing since he was thirteen years old in a number of different genres: thriller, espionage, science fiction, literary. He's the author of seven novels in the Sam Dyke Investigations series and two other non-crime works, as well as two collections of blog posts on the craft of writing. When he's not writing he enjoys reading, learning the guitar, watching movies and binge-inhaling great TV series. He's currently spending more time in France than is probably good for him. Check out his website **www.keithdixonnovels.com** or Tweet: **@keithyd6**

MARK FINE *[Mark of the Hyena]*, a self-confessed, tone-deaf music executive, was born in South Africa, However, now Los Angeles is his home. There with his two sons—and Charlie, an affectionate neighbor's dog—Mark wrote his historical fiction novel, *The Zebra Affaire*—the story of a mixed race couple and their struggle to survive under the racist regime's oppressive 1970's apartheid policies. Mark also takes a broader look at the travails of greater Africa; a topic that concerns him greatly. A charming aspect of Mark's writing is how he looks to nature—Africa's animals and wildlife—for inspiration and a solution to human shortcomings. In the process of telling the truth via the freedom fiction provides, a reviewer said, *"Mark Fine has been brave like William Faulkner in his journey of truth telling – he has simply done it with a much different kind of Southern accent."* For further info on Mark, check out these links **www.finebooks.co** and **www.MarkFineBooks.com** and you're welcome to Tweet: **@MarkFine_author**

ERIC J. GATES *[Death of a Sparrowman]* has had a curious life filled with the stuff of thriller novels. Writing Operating Systems for Supercomputers, cracking cryptographic codes under extreme pressure using only paper and pen and teaching Cyberwarfare to spies are just a few of the moments he's willing to recall. He is an ex-International Consultant who has travelled extensively worldwide, speaks several languages. His specialty, Information Technology Security, has brought him into contact with the Military and Intelligence communities on numerous occasions. He is also an expert martial artist, holding 14 black belt degrees in distinct disciplines. He has taught his skills to Police and Military personnel, as well as to the public. Eric now writes thriller novels, drawing on his experiences with the confidential and secret worlds that surround us. Visit his website at **www.ericjgates.com** for extracts, inside secrets, and a competition where you could be a character in his next book. Follow Eric J. Gates on Twitter: **@eThrillerWiter**

ULLA HÅKANSON *[Squatter]* was born and educated in Umeå, a small city by the Baltic Sea in the northern part of Sweden. As a young feisty little kid, smaller than most of her friends, she enjoyed frightening them with scary stories that she would make up. After spending four years at the Royal Institute of Technology in Stockholm, creating scientific illustrations for a Nobel prize winner in Plasma Physics, she continued her drafting career in Toronto. At age 48 she went back to college to get a commercial arts degree. Navigating through large flocks of black-clad young artists in their 20s, she subsequently

graduated and ran her own design company until retiring on Vancouver Island, British Columbia. There she rediscovered her passion for story-telling. This time by writing thrillers. After a lifetime away, she is back to her first vocation, but with a bigger audience. Ulla's first novel, *The Price of Silence*, was published by BroadPen Books in July 2013. Her next novel, a freestanding sequel to The Price of Silence, is coming out in the late fall of 2016. You are invited to visit Ulla's Amazon page.

ELIZABETH HORTON-NEWTON *[Red Queen Check]* was born and raised in New York City. She began writing when she was a child, writing stories for friends and family. In the 4th Grade at P.S. 151 in Manhattan, she wrote an essay about her dream job—she wanted to be an author. Elizabeth continued to write short stories over the following years as she raised a family. After attending Long Island University in Brooklyn, NY and East Tennessee State University, she worked in the social work field for thirteen years. She currently lives in East Tennessee with her husband, author Neil Newton, and a collection of rescued dogs and cats. Her first book *View From the Sixth Floor: An Oswald Tale* was published in October 2014; a love story that revolves around the assassination of President John Kennedy on November 22, 1963—and the ensuing conspiracy theories. This was followed in June 2015 with the release of *Riddle*, a romantic thriller about a Native American convicted of killing his high school girlfriend. Elizabeth's third novel, a somewhat erotic romance of one woman's journey through love, loss, and resolution, will be released in the fall of 2016. This mother of 4, grandmother of 5, and great grandmother of a

newly arrived boy, loves serial killers and all things horror. She has been this way since early childhood, much to her mother's dismay. Fascinated by the inner workings of the criminal mind, an interest strongly influenced by her father, she allowed her imagination to run wild in her tale for this anthology. You are invited to pay Elizabeth a visit at *Between the Beats* (**www.elizabethnnewton.com**) and her author website **www.elizabethhorton-newtonauthor.com** or connect via Twitter: **@redqueenliz**

ANITA KOVACEVIC *[Beneath]* is a multi-genre author and ESL (English Second Language) teacher. Despite being inordinately busy, Anita has published and illustrated an urban-legend novella, *The Threshold*, a light romance novel, *Average Daydreamer*, and three children's books (*Winky's Colours*, *The Good Pirate* and *Mimi Finds Her Magic*). Anita's stories and poems appear in *Inner Giant*, and recently the two *Awethology Light* collections. Anita is an avid reader, storyteller and poet, and dabbles as a songwriter and editor. Creativity feeds her soul, so there are always several teaching and writing projects that keep her on the go. She lives with her husband and children in Croatia and doesn't know the meaning of 'free time'. Despite being so busy, Anita would love to hear from you via her blog, **www.AnitasHaven.wordpress.com** or Twitter: **@Anitas_haven**

MICHELLE MEDHAT *[Angel Heart]* has had an exciting career that spans over 27 years in technology, science, education and marketing. Currently, Michelle is Director of Operations and Strategic Development at NEF: The Innovation Institute, an educational charity and professional institute that she co-founded with her husband Professor S Sam Medhat in 2004. The Institute has donated

millions of pounds to the science, engineering and technology education sector, and has helped to improve the lives of over 600,000 people. In her spare time, Michelle enjoys writing, reading, painting and singing. During her career, she has written extensively for publications, journals and newspapers, and has numerous short stories published in various anthologies. Michelle has two published books - *Connected: The Call* and *Connected: The Shift*, and she's currently working on a third in the Connected series. In doing so she literally blends gritty spy thriller with political intrigue, and a smattering of science fiction, to deliver books that are original and heart-pounding. To learn more, connect with Michelle via Twitter: **@theconnected1**

GEOFF NELDER *[Ubiquitous]* has one wife, two grown-up kids, and lives in rural England within easy cycle ride of the Welsh mountains. A former high school teacher of geography and information technology, he has had non-fiction books published on microclimates in the UK along with several articles in academic journals such as *Weather*, *Geographical Magazine* and the *Times Educational Supplement*. Geoff is a part-time journalist contributing humorous travel accounts to *Cycling World*. Having had 84 short stories published, Geoff was chosen to be the short fiction judge for the Whittaker Prize. He won first prize in the Cafe Doom short story competition in 2005 and won a commendation for a story in the Ron Hubbard Writers of the Future Competition. His humorous thriller *Escaping Reality*, (2005) was published by Brambling Books. Another thriller, *Hot Air*, (2009) received an award from an Arts Academy in the Netherlands. This was followed by his blockbuster science fiction post-apocalyptic

trilogy, *ARIA,* (2012-2015). Geoff is also an editor at *Adventure Books of Seattle*, a co-editor of science fiction magazine, *Escape Velocity*, and has for several years been a freelance editor of novels and short stories. Currently, the Rebecca Pratt Literary Agency is touting his latest work, the historical fantasy, *Xaghra's Revenge*. For Geoff's UK and USA readers please visit his Amazon Author page. Or, connect via Facebook and Twitter: **@geoffnelder**

Canadian born, **FIONA QUINN** *[A Crooked Mile]* is now rooted in the Old Dominion outside of D.C. with her husband and four children. There, she homeschools, pops chocolates, devours books, and taps continuously on her laptop. She is the creative force behind the popular blog *ThrillWriting*. Quinn writes the bestselling Lynx Series including: Kindle Scout winning novel WEAKEST LYNX as well as MISSING LYNX, CHAIN LYNX, and CUFF LYNX. She also wrote the mystery novella, MINE and co-authored CHAOS IS COME AGAIN a noir comedy. Look for her newest series STRIKE FORCE. A visit to Fiona's Amazon Author page is a treat.

Author and mother of three, **TRACI SANDERS** *[Keeping It in the Family]* has been composing poetry, songs, and children's stories since the young age of ten. In 2003, she opened her home to young children in her community offering "beyond the basics" teachings. In 2008, she was recognized by the Child Care Resource and Referral Agency as F*amily Childcare Provider of the Year* and was featured in the media. In 2010, she furthered her education by earning her Child Development Associates degree and was a recipient of the *FIRST (First Incentive for Raising Standards among Teachers) Award* presented by the Child Care

Commissioner of her state. She continues to shape the young minds of the future through her home-based childcare program. Her daily interactions with these children provide constant inspiration for her writing and she plans to continue on this path until her story has reached "The End." Traci has two goals in writing books—to help people and/or to make them feel something. To date, she has published six books. Her most recent is a paranormal romance titled, *Unsevered*, released in 2015. Her blog, *A Word with Traci* is at **www.awordwithtraci.com**.

LUBNA SENGUL *[Cold]* is the author of *The Danfians Prophecy*, a Scifi / Fantasy-Romance book. The story reflects the author's colorful imagination in almost a cinematic way, where the reader can envisage the story play out in their mind. It's almost like having one's very own movie on the go, as the lens pans through the pages of a book! Lubna is inspired by life and all the challenges that us humans have to overcome, a sentiment which is displayed in her writing. Her character development skills are a result of working with a theater company. To keep Lubna on her toes, and grounded, she can count on her supportive and beautiful family. Her favorite authors include—but not limited to—are: J.K Rowling, MC Scott (Manda Scott), Khaled Hosseini, Tim Willocks, Stephanie Meyers, Anne Rice, Virginia Andrews, Andrea Levy. A reading taste that fits into many genres, but nothing nourishes her imagination better than a good sci-fi/fantasy that has a romance element to it. You can visit Lubna's Amazon page.

*****

For more about **Readers Circle of Avenue Park**.
And to join (it is free), please visit:
www.ReadersAvenuePark.weebly.com

Printed in Poland
by Amazon Fulfillment
Poland Sp. z o.o., Wrocław